Bae Belongs to Me 2

Lock Down Publications and Ca$h
Presents
Bae Belongs to Me 2
A Novel by *Aryanna*

Lock Down Publications

P.O. Box 870494
Mesquite, Tx 75187

Visit our website @
www.lockdownpublications.com

Copyright 2019 by Bae Belongs to Me 2

First Edition May 2019
Printed in the United States of America

This is a work of fiction. Names, characters, places, and incidents either are products of the author's imagination or are used ficti- tiously. Any similarity to actual events or locales or persons, living or dead, is entirely coincidental.

Lock Down Publications
Like our page on Facebook: Lock Down Publications @
www.facebook.com/lockdownpublications.ldp
Cover design and layout by: **Dynasty Cover Me**
Book interior design by: **Shawn Walker**
Edited by: **Shawn Walker**

Stay Connected with Us!

Text **LOCKDOWN** to 22828 to stay up-to-date with new releases, sneak peaks, contests and more...

Thank you.

Dedication:

This book is forever dedicated to the crazy bitches I know!!!

Acknowledgements:

I give all glory to god for being everything and for making me everything that I am. I have to thank my better half, soulmate, and best friend for all the love and support. I couldn't do this thing called life without you, and I love you for helping me to understand that. I have to thank my little Ary with the big nose, you're my twin and I love you no matter what. I have to thank my LOYAL FANS for still rocking with me and believing in my ability to take you somewhere with my words. I got plenty ore heat in this pen for you, I promise. I have to thank my family because you are who you are, and I love you for it. Special shout out to Big Byrd! I honesty don't know what I would do without you because you're that quiet voice in th3e dark that we all need. You're that loud voice in the light that we need too! Lol! Oh, yeah, and to that ignorant nigga Moe…you had a good one champ, but you blew it.
I have to thank my LDP family for all that you do, and for continuing to chase your dreams. Steel sharpens steel! Special thanks to Cash for the time you spend mentoring me on how to better my craft and my life, you sage advice is appreciated.
Shout out to the real ones stuck behind the wall: Delvin "Polo" Henderson, Terrance "Pree" Henderson, Dwayne "squeeze" Young, Uncle Lin, and A.J. founder of H.Y.P.E (helping youth prevail everywhere). I salute the fact that you've turned your incarceration into something positive.

Keep pushing others to do that right thing, and keep doing your thing until society views you as more than your state number. It don't cost you nothing to be real, remember that when shit gets hard. Shout out to B.G from the north side of Richmond Virginia. You a rapping fool young nigga, chase your dream! Shout out to 40, just hold on bruh and it'll get better. Shout out to D #1055995, I got you! I cant forget my females stuck behind them same lines: T.N.T (little dynamite) I love you! your time is almost up, and then your best life begins. Shout out to the Beautiful disaster (Amanda). If it ain't life it ain't long, and we'll be here for you regardless. Shout out to Ashley (too tall). Stop doubting me because we both know I'm too real to be fake!! I cant forget about 1 ½ chains. No means no! lol! Before I go I gotta thank all the people in my immediate circle, no names are needed because you all know who you are, and you know that I love you.

Lastly, thank you to ALL MY HATER!! You make it hard to stay humble because I just wanna rub it in your face, but I'm gonna keep it cute…FUCK YOU.

LDP, THE GAME IS OURS!!!!

Prologue
July 2017

"Freeze!" Came the command from behind me, forcing me to turn around.

"She's got my ba—"

I never got to finish my sentence before I was lifted off of my feet. Whoever had shot me was hiding behind the multiple flashlight beams that were bouncing all around the room, so I couldn't see who it was. All I could see was Elyse's lifeless gray eyes inches from mine, and I wondered if this was the end for both of us. Were we fated to die together? And if so, what would become of our son. The silence coming from my little man was so loud in my mind that it sounded like a scream, but I knew there was nothing I could do about it. I was dying.

Aryanna

Chapter 1
Five days later

I opened my eyes slowly, taking my time to evaluate my surroundings while asking myself how the fuck I got here. My environment was a surprise, but even more surprising than that was the beautiful woman curled up in the chair beside my bed asleep. She looked so peaceful and innocent, but I wondered who she was really, and why was she here. Was it love that had her forgoing the comforts of her own bed in order to be by my side? Was it loyalty? And if so, had I given her the same loyalty? I had so many questions, and maybe she could help me answer just a few so I didn't feel completely lost and overwhelmed.

"Miss? Miss, wake up," I said gently.

Watching her eyes open slowly was like seeing the blinds open on a beautiful naked woman, who was unaware that she was being watched. I didn't know what to call the particular shade of blue looking back at me, but it was hypnotizing.

"Hey bae, how are you feeling?" she asked, unfolding from the chair.

"Bae? I'm—I'm your bae?" I asked confused.

"Of course, you are. You're my everything," she replied, holding up her wedding ring for me to see.

Immediately, I looked down at my left hand, discovering the matching diamond and platinum wedding band there. The way it sparkled under the hospital lights let me know that it was definitely real, but was the love and commitment that it symbolized just as real?

"How did we get here?" I asked.

"You don't remember?"

I shook my head sadly while looking around the hospital room again.

"Well, you were shot in the head and chest by the police almost a week ago, and the doctor put you in a coma until the swelling in your brain went down. The fact that you're awake this soon and coherent, is a miracle," she replied.

The concern on her face was touching and it showed that whoever she was that she cared about me

"Shot? What did I do to get myself shot?"

"You didn't do anything, baby, and that's why our lawyers have already filed a huge lawsuit against the Fairfax County Police Department," she said, reassuringly.

"We've got lawyers?" I asked, somewhat shocked.

"Bae, *exactly* what do you remember?"

Her question made me close my eyes in search of images that would bring any explanation to my life right now, but all I saw was darkness. There were no flashes or short films that summarized my existence, and that gave me a feeling of blind panic.

"I—I don't know who I am. I don't remember who I am," I said, shakily.

"It's okay, sweetheart, it's okay. I'm here" she replied, climbing into the bed beside me.

The way she clung to me demonstrated that she wasn't afraid of me, but maybe she should've been. No matter what she said, if the police had put two bullets in me then the odds were that I was a dangerous man. She should've been scared.

"I don't know what to do, I mean I'm literally lost in the world," I said mystified.

"Bae, all you have to do is get healthy, and I'll help you to get better. I'm your wife, your best friend and I love you more than anything in the world. I know you might not trust me yet, but you can trust that."

"I don't even know what I'm supposed to do to get healthy," I said, honestly.

"I don't even know what I'm supposed to do to get healthy." I flexed my fingers to relieve the cramping before gingerly touching my forehead.

"Well, let's ask your doctor," she replied, hitting the nurses call button.

Moments later an attractive brown skin girl came through the door, carrying a clipboard. "Look who's awake. How are you feeling, Mr. Monroe?" she asked.

"Fine, I guess. A little confused," I replied.

"Well, that's understandable, given the head trauma you suffered. Let me evaluate you really quick, and then I'll go get your doctor," she said.

I could feel the hesitation radiating from my wife's body, but eventually she got up and moved to the side so the nurse could handle her business. She never took her eyes off of us though. Nurse Robinson checked all of my vitals, asked me a series of questions, while checking my eyes and then she left.

"I know this is gonna sound crazy, what's your name?" I asked my wife.

"My name is Katrina Monroe, and your name is Ahmani."

"Ahmani? And Katrina? Well, I guess it could've been worse," I said, smiling at her.

"Trust me, there are some people with some *real* fucked up names in the world. I don't think you'll have a problem remembering mine, though."

"I shouldn't, I mean, it's…"

"Mr. Monroe, it's good to see you awake and alert. I'm Doctor Aleck Beni," a middle-aged white man said, offering me his hand to shake.

"Nice to meet you, Doctor," I replied.

"So, Nurse Robinson tells me that you're experiencing memory loss," he stated.

"Yeah, I can't remember anything beyond opening my eyes a little while ago," I confessed.

"How long will this last, Doctor?" Katrina asked.

"One can never tell when it comes to matters of the brain how long it will take to heal itself from the inside out. The fact that the bullet lodged in his frontal lobe saved his life, but it obviously stilled caused some damage. We will need to do a few cat scans to determine the extent of the damage done, but the truth is that he may never regain his memory in whole or in part," the doctor replied truthfully.

"So, I could just be a nobody for the rest of my life?" I asked softly.

"You'll *never* be a nobody, Ahmani, especially not to me," Katrina replied quickly, moving to my side and taking my hand.

I couldn't deny the comfort that I took from her gesture, even though I didn't know her.

"How does your chest feel?" The doctor asked.

So far, I hadn't had a reason to move, but now that he asked the question, I felt immediate discomfort.

"It hurts," I replied, putting my hand to the center of my chest.

I could feel the bandage there and it was sure to the touch. And it was sore to the touch

"You'll probably feel that more than the shot you took to the head, but luckily it went straight through your chest and out your back without tearing anything up. The bullet missed your spine by centimeters," he said.

"So, I won't have to do physical therapy?" I asked.

"No, the main thing that you need to do is rest. You're young and you're strong, so I believe that you'll heal nicely with plenty of rest. I'm sorry, but that means you'll be doing the late-night feedings for now, Mrs. Monroe," he said, smiling at Katrina.

"Late night feedings?" I asked, confused.

Katrina and the doctor exchanged a quick look that I didn't understand, forcing me to squeeze her hand in mine to get her attention.

"There's a lot you two probably want to discuss, so I'll come back after your cat scan. It should take place in about thirty minutes," the doctor informed us, backing slowly out of the room.

"I know there's a lot that I don't know, but if you love me like you say you do, then you'll help me fill in the gaps," I said, looking at her expectantly.

"You're right, I'm just worried about overwhelming you. You do deserve to know about your son before anything else."

"My son? I have a so—son?" I stammered, unable to stop my eyes from filling up with tears.

"Yes, you do, and he's named after you."

"How old is he? Where is he? What does he look like?" I asked, firing my questions rapidly.

In response, Katrina pulled a phone from her pocket and moved her fingers across the screen until she found what she was looking for. Once she put the phone in my hand and I got a look at the tiny little brown body filling up the screen, my tears immediately fell.

"He's so beautiful," I said, fighting not to openly sob.

"Yeah, he is and he's a fighter, too, because he was a little premature."

"These pictures show him to be no more than a week old. You had our baby less than a week ago?" I asked, looking her over from head to toe.

Despite the fact that she had a sweat suit on it was still easy to tell how thick she was, but it was toned and not baby fat.

"That's where the story gets complicated, bae, but I'll explain."

Listening to her tell me about my ex and our relationship, and then how Katrina had *still* showed up when my ex couldn't find me to help her deliver my son made me look at her in a new light. She may not have been able to save Elyse's life, but I still had my son.

"You're incredible. Not only did you save my son's life, but somehow you found it in your heart to forgive me for cheating? How do I deserve someone like you?" I asked sincerely.

"We're soulmates, Ahmani, meant to be together for all eternity, so nothing will come in between that. I forgave you for your past because I know no one is perfect. I'm certainly not."

"I find that hard to believe. I mean you're beautiful, kind, understanding, loving. That sounds perfect to me," I said.

"Well, baby, as long as you think so that's all that matter's," she replied, getting back into the bed with me.

"I feel bad that little Ahmani won't know his birth mother, but at least he'll have the love of the woman who helped bring him into the world."

"Yes, he will, and so will you," she said, kissing me tenderly.

I may not have remembered anything, but my body absolutely knew this woman because my response was immediate. The softness of her lips and the faint taste of chocolate on her tongue pulled me into her orbit and for a moment, everything, other than our joined mouths, ceased to exist. The spell she put me under was so intense that I never felt her moving until she was under the covers with me, pushing my hospital gown up.

"Baby h—hold up we can't…"

"We can do whatever we wanna do," she insisted, throwing her leg over me and straddling me in one quick motion.

The fact that I could feel the heat of her skin from her thighs, signifying that she was naked from the waist down, told me that my protests were useless. As she took a firm hold of my dick and guided it inside of her warm, wet, tight pussy, her lips found mine and we shared a kiss that shot electricity through me. The pain in my chest was real, but still I grabbed two handfuls of her plump ass and pulled her toward me until she had all of me locked in her walls.

"I—I don't wanna hurt you," she whispered against my lips.

"Nothing that feels this good could hurt, besides, you could never hurt me," I replied, raising my legs slightly so she was taking the dick from an angle.

Our pace was slow and deliberate, and she rode my dick like she'd known me in another lifetime. The way our anatomy throbbed together was indicative of our wants and needs harmonizing like a beautiful love song, and I was praying that the music didn't stop. I fought through the pain to pull her toward me faster, motivated by the moans echoing from her mouth to mine. Suddenly her body tensed up from the inside out and a sigh of ecstasy rolled off of her tongue as she was rocked by an orgasm.

I didn't know it was possible until it happened, but her climax made her pussy tighter and threatened my sanity. Still I pushed her to ride on because the ghost I was chasing was just beyond my field of vision.

"I love you, Ahmani!" she said passionately.

Her declaration made me fight through the pain and lift my hips, creating a combination of lightning and thunder that left us both breathless.

Within minutes, she was cumming again, but this time I knew fulfillment as intimately as she did. The smell of our sex and our ragged breathing filled the room around us, but we were both wrapped up in the high of satisfaction.

"Was it always that good?" I asked, looking up into her sparkling, blue eyes.

"Mmhmm. Even when it's a quickie, it's amazing."

"Damn! I hope that means we fuck a lot," I said, smiling.

"Oh, we did before and we *definitely* will now because I need it."

"Oh, you *need* it, do you?" I asked playfully.

"Absolutely. Being pregnant makes me hornier."

Chapter 2
Five weeks later

I thought I'd known panic when I woke up in a hospital and couldn't figure out how I got there, but thanks to Katrina that feeling was short lived. The *real* panic set in when I made her guide me through the mine field that was my memory or lack thereof.

She may not have been able to fill in the gaps for the first twenty years of my life, but based on her description of the last year, I'd been living in a fucking movie! The late-nights we stayed up talking pushed me through every range of emotion from anger to grief, and back to anger. I wasn't just angry for the shit me and my family had had to endure, I was also seeing red about the shit my wife had gone through, and was going through.

Not only was the mufucka who had killed her parents trying to blame her for it but from what Katrina had told me, he was actually trying to say she had *my* family killed!

I knew that was bullshit from the moment she spoke the words, especially since the way they were killed signaled to me that it was my fault. I'd carry that guilt with me forever, even if I couldn't remember the enemies I'd made to deserve that type of wrath and revenge.

Even with me knowing the truth in my heart, Katrina had still shown me the findings from the private investigator she'd hired to prove her innocence. Rich people were never as clever as they thought, and Aaron Charles was the latest example of that because of the money trail he'd left that led to his hired gun. Nobody could find him, though, but Aaron was gonna pay for all sins like Jesus Christ.

"I thought I'd find you down here," she said, coming down the stairs into the basement.

"Yeah, I was just trying to clear my mind, and shooting seems to help," I replied, lowering the Glock .45 to my side.

"I remember when we first got together you didn't know how to shoot."

"I didn't?" I asked, looking down range at the tight grouping of holes I'd put in the target.

"I know what it's hard to believe now, but you really didn't. I didn't tell you before because I wanted to see if your body would simply take over, and it looks like it had."

"Yeah, I'm not sure if that's a good thing or a bad thing, I just know that I have to be able to protect what I love," I said sincerely.

"Does that include me?" she asked seductively, taking the gun from my hand, while offering me her lips to sample.

"Of course, It does, Mrs. Monroe, and not just because you're carrying our child either. No one, and I mean *no one* will ever hurt you as long as I'm alive. The only man to cause you pain will be me," I replied, biting her lip and then sucking on it.

"Mmm, well, how about you inflict some of that pain now in the shower because we gotta get going."

"Whatever you say," I replied, smacking her ass hard.

The smile she gave me was dazzling as she took a couple steps back from me. Without warning, she turned her eyes down range, lifted the gun in her hand and fired off a quick five shots. Her grouping was just as tight as mine, but all of her shots were head shots.

"Nice." I was impressed.

"Who do you think taught you, bae? I'll meet you upstairs," she replied, smiling while handing me my gun back.

I waited until she was gone before I emptied the rest of the clip into the target and then reloaded. Despite Katrina's statement about my lack of gun play before her and I became a couple, but since coming home from the hospital I still only felt safe when I had one within reach, so I never left home without it. Once I had an extra clip, I made my way upstairs and picked out my clothes for the day.

Tossing everything on the bed, I followed the sounds of running water into the bathroom where I found Katrina's soapy, wet and waiting. The way her 5'0ft, 155lb frame was put together turned me on no matter what she was wearing, but seeing her naked was always something different. The thickness of her thighs and ass, the way her firm titties begged to be sucked and the pussy that I knew was pretty, pink and tight all combined to make my mouth dry at times like this.

She was something special. As soon as I opened the shower door, she leaped into my arms from out of the fog and the battle for sexual fulfillment was officially on!

One hour and multiple positions later, we lay on the shower floor wearing smiles of satisfaction despite the journey of pleasure and pain.

"Can't get enough of your loving," I admitted.

"Mmm, me either, but we don't have to stop because we've got forever together."

"Indeed, we do. As much as I want to, though, I know I can't use sex to avoid what I need to do," I said, getting shakily to my feet and pulling her off of the floor.

We quickly washed ourselves before getting out of the shower to get dressed. Since I finished up before her, I went to peak in on my son in the nursery that was down the hall from our bedroom.

He was a lively one when he was awake, but I loved to watch him sleep. I crept up to his crib and just stood there for a moment, watching his tiny chest move up and down, up and down. From the first time I'd held him, I'd vowed he'd never know the pain and evils of the world because I'd be there to stand in front of him. I'd give my life for him a thousand times over in a thousand different ways, just the same as I would his sibling that was on the way. That was my job and my right as a father and nothing would get in the way of that.

"Bae," Katrina whispered from behind me.

I turned to find her wearing the matching denim skirt to the Black Billionaire jeans I was rocking, a pair of low-top all white Air Force Ones and a white t-shirt. In her hand, she had my gun and extra clip, which she was holding out for me to take. I turned back to my son, kissed my fingers, and gently placed them on his forehead before backing out of his room.

"Where's the nanny?" I asked, tucking the pistol in the waist of my jeans and putting the clip in my pocket.

"She's in the kitchen, making Ahmani's bottle for when he wakes up."

The good thing about having money was the ability to hire the best when it came to live-in help, but I was still determined that I would spend more time with my kids than anybody.

"Let's go," I said, leading the way downstairs to the garage.

Even though I didn't like driving because I didn't know where I was going half of the time, Katrina insisted that I do it. In her opinion, there was no other way for me to learn my way around. She'd made it even harder for me to refuse by exchanging the old Porsche 911 she'd given me for a brand-new silver 2018 Porsche 911 GT. I loved driving that beast, which was why I grabbed those keys off of the peg board once we got into the garage.

"What time is the appointment?" I asked.

"In thirty minutes, and if we're late it's your fault for fucking me too good."

Her statement made me chuckle, as I got behind the wheel and fired the engine. Once I had us out of the garage and beyond the gates of out exclusive community, I mashed the gas and ate up the road.

"It's-it's okay if we're a llittle late," she said, gripping the arm rest hard enough to make her knuckles white.

Of course, I ignored her comment and focused on navigating the road.

Twenty-five minutes later we slid to a stop in front of her lawyer's office.

"With time to spare," I said, smiling.

The look she gave me made me laugh out loud. We spent a good twenty minutes going over and signing our newly drafted will before we were back on the road headed to our next destination.

"Do you really think all of that was necessary?" I asked.

"Yes, baby, I do. I mean our lives are proof enough that anything can happen, and I never want our kids to struggle."

"Shit, that's virtually an impossibility with your net worth," I stated.

"*Our* net worth. You're my husband, remember?"

"That's not something that I'll ever forget again, sweetheart, but either way a quarter of a billion dollars is a lot of fucking money," I said seriously.

"It is, and honestly that not even all of it. There's money in Geneva, Switzerland and the Grand Caymans. There's more money than you and I could run through in two lifetimes, but the important thing is that our kids are straight no matter what happens."

"Well, thanks to you they will be. The fact that you included Ahmani Junior in everything means a lot to me, too," I said, taking her hand in mine and kissing it.

"Of course, I included him. He's my son, too, and I love him."

"And I love you," I stated, smiling.

"I'm kinda gonna need you to prove that, sir."

"And how would you like me to prove that, Mrs. Monroe?"

"You can start by feeding a bitch, I mean, I *am* eating for two," she replied, rubbing her barely there baby bump.

She was almost five months along according to her last doctors visit, but she didn't look it. She damn sure ate like it, though!

"What do you wanna eat?" I asked.

The look she gave me was full of untold mischief, causing me to shake my head and smile ruefully.

"I swear your ass is insatiable woman!"

"My ass, my mouth and my pussy," she replied, pulling my hand to her mouth so she could suck my fingers.

"Katrina don't start."

"Oh, alright. To answer your question, though, I want a steak and cheese sub from Quiznos," she said.

"Six inch or foot long?"

"Now see, you tell me not to start and then you ask me some shit like that," she replied, hitting me playfully.

"My bad, bae. Why don't you just decide when we get there, okay?"

"Mmhmm. You keep up with the bullshit and I'ma suck your dick again while you're driving," she threatened.

No duded probably would've took her words as being Most dudes probably would've taken her words as being threatened with a good time, but I vividly recalled me putting her H2 Hummer in a ditch the last time that happened. I'd felt regret for fucking up her truck, but I was *terrified* I'd done something to jeopardize the baby inside of her.

"We not even 'bout to try that shit again, so don't even think it," I said seriously.

We continued to talk shit and joke up until, and even after, we'd gotten our lunches.

The moment we cruised into Manassas, Virginia the seriousness of why we were here grabbed ahold of both of us.

Since my discharge from the hospital, Katrina had brought me back to Manassas on several occasions, explaining that this was where her and I had grown up. It was hard to believe we came from different, yet similar, worlds given the money she came from.

She'd run her whole life story down to me. The amazing thing was her patience when it came to helping me put my own story together. She'd gone with me to a storage unit that I'd apparently gotten after my mom and siblings were killed, and she'd sat there with me while I poured over box after box of memories, with tears blinding me the entire time.

It helped to know where I came from, but it hurt to come back here just the same. I pulled over at a local florist and bought a dozen roses before we continued our journey to the cemetery. This had been the one place I'd put off coming to, but we both agreed it was the place I needed to visit the most.

"Are you ready?" she asked, once I brought the car to a stop in the cemetery parking lot.

"I guess."

"It's okay, baby, I'm right here with you," she said, reassuringly.

With this knowledge in mind, I took a deep breath and stepped out of the car. Katrina followed my lead, carrying the flowers and taking my hand once we were walking along the gravel path leading up the hill. Long before now she'd explained to me that she'd had to make all the burial and funeral arrangements because I'd been too distraught to do anything.

She'd spared no expense and actually had my loved ones buried in a mausoleum.

As we made it to the top of the hill, I saw the structure she'd described and my steps faltered a little.

"It's okay, baby, I'm *right here*," she repeated, squeezing my hand tighter.

Squaring my shoulders, I opened the door and allowed her to step into the gloom first. The sound of voices echoed throughout the building, but I didn't think anything of it until Katrina suddenly stopped moving forward.

"What is it, babe?" I asked, looking at the two people standing a few feet from us.

She didn't say anything, but her eyes stayed glued to the man and woman in front of us. It was on the tip of my tongue to question Katrina again, but at that exact moment the couple turned toward us and the look on the dude's face was easy to understand.

"You conniving bitch!" he declared, reaching behind his back.

Out of sheer instinct I pulled my wife behind me, while reaching for the pistol underneath my shirt.

"Nigga, you must be out your mind to pull a gun on me," he said, clutching his own gun at his side.

"If you raise that pistol in the direction of me or my wife I'ma show you just how out of my mind I am," I vowed seriously.

"Ahmani, what are you *doing*?!" The girl standing beside him asked.

Her calling me by my name startled me, but I tried not to let it show.

"I know you?" I asked, casting a fleeting glance in her direction.

"Know me? Nigga is that supposed to be some kind of joke?" she asked with hostility on her tongue.

"This don't seem to be the time for shits and giggles, so if I know you, then you better be clear about that shit because right now my focus is on this nigga who obviously wants to shoot my pregnant wife," I said.

"Pregnant?" The girl echoed softly.

"Hold up, hold up, time out. Nigga, are you *seriously* standing there saying you don't know either of us?" Dude asked skeptically.

My response was to cock the hammer on my gun because my patience for the bullshit had just about ran out.

"Wait! Ahmani, look at me, it's *Amee* and I've known you since we were kids. You, me and Black Boy grew up together," she said, stepping in between me and him, while holding her hands up to keep us from shooting.

For a moment, I looked down into her mesmerizing green eyes, and then up into his brown ones. They were definitely older, but there was a familiarity from some pictures I'd found in storage.

"Katrina, is she telling the truth?" I asked, still not lowering my gun.

"You do know them, but I don't know how close you are to them," Katrina replied.

"Bitch, what type of game are you playing?" Amee asked, trying to look past me.

"Why don't you remember us?" Black Boy asked, with a curious look on his face.

"Because I got shot in the head by the cops a month and a half ago," I replied.

He stared at me for a few more moments before nodding his head and slowly putting his gun away. As a show of good faith, I lowered mine to my side, but it stayed cocked and ready.

"So that story was true, you really did get shot by the cops?" he asked.

"Yeah, I did," I replied.

"Ahmani, you need to listen to me because…"

"Amee, don't. He'd obviously been through a lot and all that we can do is give him time," Black Boy said.

I could see clearly the displeasure on Amee's beautiful face, but the look that they exchanged kept her quiet.

"I'm glad you're alive," Amee emotionally said, giving me a hug.

The sincerity with which she spoke told me she really did care about me, and for that reason I hugged her back. When she pulled back, I felt her hand slip into my pocket, but the look she gave me silenced any questions I was about to ask.

"We'll let you pay your respects in peace," Black Boy said, taking Amee by the arm and ushering her out.

The look in both of their eyes said there was a lot to say and despite out almost violent reintroduction, I was more than curious. What did they know that I didn't?

Chapter 3

The moonlight peeking through the window only enhanced Katrina's beauty, making it impossible not to watch her sleeping beside me. The way her black hair fanned out across her pillow in stark contrast to her milky white skin was sexy to me, and I showed her just how much by waking her up twice with the dick already. It was scary to me. I'd showed her just how much by walking her up twice with the dick already.

Still I felt a restless energy that I couldn't put into words. I definitely knew the cause of it though, and I'd been debating with myself for the past forty-five minutes about what I was gonna do about it. I probably shouldn't have been doing shit at 3:15 a.m. except sleep, but it was evident I was about to ignore that truth because I was already sliding from beneath the comforter.

As quietly as I could, I grabbed my clothes and shoes before I tiptoed into the hallway. Once there, I quickly got dressed, ran downstairs to grab my gun and found myself sitting behind the wheel of my Porsche five minutes after leaving my wife's bed. Reaching into my jeans' pocket I pulled out the phone Amee had slipped me earlier, rereading the one-line text that came through right before midnight.

Come see me.

I hadn't responded earlier, but now I shot a text asking for her address. Part of me worried that she would be fast asleep by now, but thirty seconds later a reply came in the form of the information I'd requested.

Without delay I opened my door, put my car in neutral, and used all of my 6'2", 250lb frame to push my car backwards. Once I had momentum, I pulled the door closed, and let the car coast as far as it could before firing up the engine and racing off into the night.

A little less than an hour later, I was creeping through Georgetown South Housing projects, with my gun in my hand ready to shoot anything posing a threat. When I pulled up out front, I text Amee and a few seconds later, I saw her open the door. I locked up my car and quickly made my way to her, keeping my gun pressed tightly against my leg but still ready for whatever.

"It seems like the last few times I've seen you you've had a gun on you, and that's more than I can remember in our entire lives," she said, stepping aside so I could come in.

"Yeah, well getting shot made me think about the importance of the second amendment."

"The second amendment? You *do* know that you're a convicted felon, right?" Amee asked, closing and locking the door.

"My wife mentioned something about that, but I'm sure that's not why you wanted to see me," I replied, taking a seat on her couch.

The house was small and somewhat cluttered, but not in a messy way. You could tell that a kid lived here because there was a bike and some skates in one corner, a basketball and football in another. It felt like a home, though, and that's what mattered.

"I wanted to see you because I love you, Ahmani, and I'm worried about you."

"You love me?" I asked, looking her up and down in the oversized t-shirt she had on.

"You sure you lost your memory?" she asked, smiling.

"That's not something anyone would play with, but why do you ask?"

"Because you're looking at me the same way you've looked at me our whole lives," she replied, chuckling.

"I may be married, but that don't mean I can't appreciate a beautiful woman."

"Boy, please, I've got on a t-shirt, no makeup and my hair is in a messy ass ponytail. Ain't nothing beautiful about that," she said.

"Let's agree to disagree for the moment, but we'll get back to that topic. Tell me what is on your mind," I said, gesturing for her to take a seat beside me.

I could feel her nervous energy as she sat down, but I didn't feel like it was coming from my presence.

"So, you really don't remember *anything*?" she asked.

"I've had help putting bits and pieces together, mainly the last year, though. Katrina and I have only been together that long."

"What do you know about her?" Amee asked carefully.

"Everything. She told me her whole life story all the way up to the point that she helped deliver my son."

Despite the fact that she was asking more questions about my wife then me, I wasn't alarmed. My instincts told me that I could trust her.

"What about her parents?" she asked.

"I know about their murder, me being caught up in the bullshit and the dude responsible trying to blame her. She even told me about him trying to say she had my family killed, but I saw proof of his guilt," I replied.

"Proof? She had proof that the mufucka they got locked up killed your mom and siblings?"

"Yeah. She already turned it over to the cops, so dude is going on death row unless I find a way to get him first," I said seriously.

"Wow. I don't know what to say."

"No offense, but you don't seem like the type to run out of words," I said, smiling.

"Shut up!" she replied, hitting me on the arm playfully.

"I'm just saying! On a serious note, though, if you and I grew up together, then you can fill in all the gaps that I'm missing, right?"

"I can try. Honestly, I'm just so happy that you're alive," she replied emotionally.

I could see the tears in her eyes and it touched me, making me put my gun down and open my arms to her. Without hesitation, she folded herself up in my embrace and cried softly. I knew there was no need for words so I didn't speak. I simply held my friend.

"This is embarrassing," she said, after a while.

"It shouldn't be, not if we're as close as you say we are."

"Oh, we're this close, but I don't cry in front of *nobody*," she stated firmly.

"So, I'm back to being nobody? Thanks a lot," I said sarcastically.

"Boy, you know what I mean!"

When she looked up at me, her eyes were alight with laughter, which was better than the sadness that had tried to swallow her a short time ago. Somehow her beauty was enhanced, too, and that made me follow the impulse in my mind telling me to kiss her.

Her lips were as soft as they looked, but I felt her whole body freeze up instantly. Part of me said pull back, but my instincts made me slowly slip my tongue in between her lips to see what she would do. Hesitantly, our tongues touched, and then they explored and finally they danced like the only two people left at the party. Despite her eluding to the fact that we'd never crossed that line, she tasted familiar and I just let my body flow with the moment. Before I knew it, I pulled her completely onto my lap and my hands were under her shirt, caressing her ass through her lace boy shorts.

"My bedroom is in the back," she whispered.

That was all I needed to hear before I picked her up and carried her down the hallway, kicking the door closed behind us. I laid her down gently on the bed and then took her shirt off of her. My kisses started at her neck and moved steadily downward, heating her flesh at each place I paused. Across her collarbone and down in between her titties I ventured, before kissing every inch of both titties. I could hear the rush of her breathing, but it suddenly stopped when my tongue made lazy circles around her nipple before I sucked it into my mouth. I mimicked my actions with her other nipple, loving the feeling of her body coming alive and her heartbeat increasing.

As I continued moving downward kissing her stomach, I pulled her panties down and off. When I resumed kissing, I started with the inside of her thighs, altering between the wetness of my lips and the pinch of my teeth from a soft bite.

"Oh, shit," she moaned weakly when I finally introduced my lips to hers.

With the speed of a snake, my tongue darted in between her pussy lips, collecting drops of her nectar for me to savor.

"Don't tease me," she begged.

I pushed a finger deep inside her tight pussy at the same time that my tongue found her clit, and the result was a strangled scream accompanied by her back arching. I moved my finger in and out of her slow and steady, but my tongue was flickering across her clit with the speed and precision of a seasoned boxer.

The first wave of orgasm gripped her within minutes, and I drank her like ice cold water on a blistering summer day. While the tremors of climatic aftershock took hold of her body, I quickly shed my clothing and climbed on the bed and in between her legs.

"Ahhh—Ahmani!" she moaned passionately when I slammed my dick completely inside of her.

I gave her two strokes like that before throwing one of her legs on my shoulder and digging deeper. This pushed her beyond words and made her cum instantly. Her pussy was so wet, but it was tight enough to make a nigga fall in love. Knowing this didn't make me stop or slow down. I just kept pounding her with strokes that made her eyes roll.

When she came again, I lost control and before I knew it, I was blinded by the most beautiful light of ecstasy. I stayed on top of her and inside of her until my dick stopped throbbing with the intensity of my hearts beat.

"You sure we've never done that?" I asked, trying to catch my breath.

"Nah. I would've remembered that."

I laid down next to her, unsure of what to do next. It felt natural to cuddle with her, so I pulled her up onto my chest and held her close.

"If I would've known that it would be that good, I would've *never* fucked with your cousin," she said.

"My cousin?"

"Damn, I keep forgetting that you don't remember. Is it okay if we talk now or are you planning to do something else magical to me?" she asked.

"Let's talk first and see where that leads."

We laid there and I listened to her talk until the sun came up, only pausing when she had to get her son up and out the door for school. After that, we continued our conversation in the shower, where I learned that Amee *definitely* had a head on her shoulders, before we made it back to the living room.

"You really do know me, huh?" I asked.

"Yeah, but I definitely learned more about you," she replied, laughing.

"I don't know how that happened, but it felt right."

"Yeah it did, didn't it? And now I'm gonna ruin it by saying some shit that I know you don't wanna hear," she said somberly.

"Okay…"

"You need to be careful around your wife. I know you think you know her like the back of your hand, but I promise you that you don't. I'm not saying this because I want you for myself, I'm saying it because I want you to live a long, healthy life," she said seriously.

"I don't believe there's any malicious intent behind what you're saying, so I'll keep it in mind as food for thought, okay?"

"Okay, I guess," she reluctantly replied.

"Now give me a hug so that I can get out of here," I said, standing up and pulling her to her feet.

We shared a long embrace and then an equally long kiss that had me wanting to carry her back to her bedroom. I knew that I had to get back home though. When I released her I pulled her phone out of my pocket and gave it back to her, along with some money.

"Don't take this the wrong way because-."

"Boy shut up. Giving me money is what you would do even if I hadn't just put this good pussy on you," she said smiling.

I gave her another quick hug, tucked my gun in the waist of my jeans and walked out the front door. It was a beautiful morning and I had some pep in my step, but no sooner had the door closed behind me I heard the sound of a shotgun slide being racked.

"You must think shit sweet, huh? You gonna pull a gun on me and then come to my hood nigga?"

I turned to my right to find Black Boy standing a few feet away in between Amee's house and the one next to it, with a chrome Mossberg aimed at me.

"Amee told me that you were crazy, but she also said we were brothers. Is that true?"

"You tell me," he said, not relaxing his grip on his gun in the slightest.

I could look in his eyes and tell that he'd pulled a trigger or two in his day, and it didn't necessarily matter who'd been on the other end of the barrel. The type of action wasn't for us though.

"I found pictures of you, me and Amee in my moms stuff, from back when we were younger. Yeah, we're brothers, so why don't you say what you really need to say because you ain't gonna shoot me," I said, confidently.

He held the gun on me for a few more seconds before lowering it and smirking at me.

"I would tell you to watch your back because your wife is treacherous, but I'll be watching your back. She won't see me coming."

Chapter 4

"Something smells good in here," I said, walking into the kitchen from the garage.

"Yeah it does. I had to get up and feed myself since you were nowhere around," Katrina replied, giving me a brief look that said a lot.

If I hadn't picked it up in her tone, the way she stared at me with her lip curled was displeasure in English and Spanish. We'd had practically no disagreements since I woke up in the hospital, so a part of me was curious to see how this was about to play out.

"Did you miss me?" I asked, moving up behind her and placing my hands on the black, silk robe covering her body.

She immediately stepped away from me, taking the pan in her hand to her plate sitting on the counter and adding her eggs to the bacon and toast that was already waiting. The temperature in the house was comfortable, almost like a sunny day indoors, but the temperature around her was hovering just above freezing.

"I guess that means you *didn't* miss me," I said, going to the refrigerator and grabbing the carton of orange juice.

"Use a glass, you're not in the projects anymore," she said, stopping me with the carton half way to my mouth.

I waited until she'd taken a seat at the kitchen counter and looked at me before I slowly put the juice container to my lips and drank from it.

"That's good juice," I stated, before burping loudly.

The look she was giving me now was several degrees colder than the one when I first came in, but it wasn't enough to dissuade my curiosity.

"Is little Ahmani okay?" I asked.

"Yes."

"Okay, well, if I'm not mistaken you *did* text me and tell me to come home now, which led me to believe that something was wrong. So, are you gonna tell me what it is or continue giving me attitude?" I asked.

The fire in her eyes was instantaneous, but it was sexy to behold, and it was giving me naughty ideas about how we could make up after this.

"Where were you, Ahmani?"

"I couldn't sleep, so I took a shower and went for a drive," I replied.

"A drive, huh? Any specific destination in mind?" she asked sarcastically.

I felt like this question was an insult to my intelligence because even without having all my memories, I'd still be smart enough to know that a 2018 Porsche came with one hell of a GPS system. I also knew that all women came with a little insecurity, so there was no way I'd put it past my wife not to track my movements.

"Actually, I wanted to go back to me and my mom's old neighborhood to see if any memories came back."

"And did they?" she inquired curiously.

"No, but I managed to talk to a few people who've known me and my family for years. They gave me a feel for the type of people we were."

"I see. One of those people you talked to was probably your friend, Amee too, huh?" she asked.

The way Amee's name came out of her mouth allowed me to damn near see the jealousy that it was coated in, but I simply smiled.

"Yes, baby, Amee was someone I spoke to. Along with her son, her sister, Black Boy and some neighbors who'd lived in the same houses for twenty-five years or more," I said, putting the juice back in the fridge before walking over to her.

She didn't say anything else, in fact, she did her best to ignore me as she ate her food. I gave her a full thirty seconds before I pushed my pants and boxers down to my ankles. She didn't look directly at my dick, but I could tell by the slight twitching of her left eye that she absolutely knew that mufucka was out.

"Look at me, Katrina."

My request didn't earn me a glance, which told me that it was time to try a different approach. Without warning, I grabbed a fistful of her hair and swiftly pulled her off of the stool she'd been sitting on.

"I told you to look at me," I growled, bringing my face inches from her.

"Ow! Ah! Ahmani you're…"

"Stop talking and *look at me*," I demanded, forcing her to kneel in front of me.

"I'm looking!"

"Good, you see this dick?" I asked, grabbing it with my other hand and tapping her on the nose with it.

She didn't verbally respond, but that fire in her eyes was now a raging inferno. I was okay with that because I could see that the added gasoline was sexual desire.

"Does this dick smell like another woman?" I asked, pushing the head of it into her nostrils.

Still she said nothing, but she did sniff.

"Does this dick *taste* like another woman?" I asked, moving it until it was sitting snugly up against her soft lips.

She stared up at me for a long five seconds before opening her mouth wide, and letting me visit the back of her throat. When she turned the suction on, I had to fight to stay focused. Amee's head had been fire, but there were absolutely no words for the things Katrina could do with her mouth. Reluctantly, I had to pull my dick free of her jaws.

"The answer to both of those questions is no, and I know that because this dick belongs to you. I would appreciate if you would act like you know that, too," I said, pulling her back to her feet, kissing her quickly and turning her loose.

With that done, I pulled my pants and boxers up before going back to the refrigerator and pulling out what I needed to make me an omelet. I could feel her eyes on me, but I didn't look at her or say a word, and eventually she climbed back on the stool to finish eating. I was halfway done making my breakfast before she spoke again.

"When I woke up and I couldn't find you in the house I got scared."

"Scared of what, bae?" I asked gently.

"Everything. Scared of being in this big house by myself. Scared that you were leaving and never coming back..."

"Sweetheart, you haven't mentioned any problems we've had, other than my infidelities, so what would make you think that I would leave you?" I asked.

"I don't know, Ahmani! I mean, I'm pregnant and my hormones are all over the place. I've never loved anyone the way that I love you, and I almost lost you once before. I can't go through that again," she replied, shaking her head sadly.

"Baby, I'm not going anywhere until the good Lord says that it's my time and since I survived a head shot, I'd say that it's a safe bet he's not ready for me, yet. You should already know that you have absolutely no reason to fear me leaving you because I love you too much and I owe you too much."

"Ahmani, you don't owe me any..."

"Shhh, I don't want to argue, especially because you can't win. I owe you and I promise to repay that debt no matter what. In the meantime, will you please just let me love you?" I asked, kissing her passionately.

"I'm not dumb enough to argue with you wanting to do that. When did you become so forceful, though?"

"You mean, I wasn't always the take charge type?" I asked.

"I don't know maybe you were, but you ain't *never* handled me like you did earlier."

I slowly parted her thighs with my hand and stuck two fingers in her pussy to verify what I already knew.

"It turned you on, too," I said, licking my fingers slowly.

"Mmhmm. Now I need you to scratch this itch for me."

"I would *love* to, bae, but we've got shit to do," I replied, backing smoothly out of her embrace.

"Unuh Ahmani, you *cannot* leave me this horny! How are you gonna torture your pregnant wife like that?" she asked, giving me her best sexy pout.

"Go Upstairs and get dressed, and let the nanny know that we'll be gone for a while," I said, going back to making my breakfast.

She tried to entice me by opening up her robe to reveal her beautiful nakedness, but I simply smiled at her and kept right on cooking. After a few minutes, she took the hint and made her way upstairs, allowing me to breathe a sigh of relief for the gamble I'd taken. I knew if I would've seemed unsure of myself it only would've allowed her suspicions and insecurities to grow roots, so I had to be two parts confident and one part arrogant.

With Katrina out of the room, I took the time to send Amee a message and tell her much I enjoyed out time together. Her response was immediate in the form of hearts and kissy face emojis, which made me smile.

I quickly erased both texts, and then I sat down to eat. By the time I finished my food, I cleaned up the kitchen behind both of us.

Katrina was breezing back into the room looking like new money. The black and gold silk Gucci dress that stopped at mid-thigh was holding her as closely as I did. The matching Gucci belt showed just how tiny her waist was, and how fat that ass was she was dragging behind her. The all-black Gucci sneakers brought it together, but the thing that caught my eye the most was the gold cross resting snugly against her firm titties.

"Is that my cross? The one that you said my mom gave me?" I asked.

"Yeah, it is. You haven't worn it since the funeral so I figured you wouldn't mind."

"I don't mind. You look *amazing* by the way," I said, looking her over from head to toe once again.

"Thank you. You didn't say where we were going, so I thought that I should look good and be comfortable."

"Mission accomplished. Let me change really quick, and we'll get on the move," I said.

I ran upstairs and quickly threw on some stonewashed black Billionaire jeans, my butter colored Timbs and fresh white t-shirt. Once I was sure I had everything I needed, I made my way back down to the kitchen, where I found Katrina impatiently waiting.

"Are you driving, or am I?" she asked.

"I got this, I'll be your chauffeur, bae."

"Okay, mister chauffeur, just try to keep the car on all four wheels this time," she said seriously.

I tried not to laugh, but I couldn't because the memory of our trip to the lawyer's office was fresh in my mind. I pulled out my phone and sent a quick text message before following Katrina into the garage and climbing into the driver's seat.

"So, are you gonna tell me where we're going?" she asked.

"No, but don't worry it'll be fun."

The look on her face said I better be telling the truth, especially since I'd denied her the dick. I got us on the road headed toward our first stop, and it wasn't long before she figured out what direction we were headed in.

"Are we really going back to Manassas?" she asked, obviously less than thrilled.

"Katrina, do you trust me?"

"Bae, you know I trust you, it's just that it's not safe…"

"Wherever I'm at you're safe, understand? I got you like nobody in this *world* got you, and that's a promise that I'ma give my life to keep," I vowed, looking over at her.

"Ahmani, I don't doubt you, but I don't want to lose you even at the cost of saving my own life. I love you more than my life."

Her words were touching and I took her hand in mine, hoping I could soothe her that way. We rode just like that until we pulled up at our first stop a half an hour later.

"No, we're *not,* bae! Are we really about to do what I think we're about to do?" She asked excitedly.

"Well, that depends. I know what *I'm* about to do, but whether or not you follow my lead is your decision," I replied, opening the door and stepping out of the car.

She quickly followed my lead and was at the door to the building before I could open it for her.

"Good morning and welcome to Fryed Ink. Do you have an appointment?" The receptionist asked.

"Yes, under the name Ahmani Monroe," I replied.

"Okay, sir, I see you reserved two separate artists. Are you getting two sleeves done at once or…"

"No, one artist is for me," Katrina spoke up, with a smile that lit up her whole face.

"Okay, do you two know what you want to get?" The receptionist asked.

"I do," I said.

"As do I," Katrina agreed.

"Alright, well, if you'll just follow me," the receptionist instructed, leading us into the back of the tattoo shop.

We were shown to chairs that sat only a few feet apart, which allowed us to really share this experience together.

"Baby, how did you know I wanted to get matching tattoos?" Katrina asked, once we were seated and waiting.

"I can't say that I actually *knew* you wanted to do this, but based on the time that we've spent together I figured anything announcing our commitment to each other to the world would be okay."

"It's more than okay. I love it."

We never got to talk about this before our lives got completely crazy, but I've *been* wanting your name on me. It wouldn't even matter if you didn't get mine because I *know* that you belong to me," she said, growing more excited with each passing second.

I loved the way her eyes lit up over something so simple. I mean some people would consider scarring your body for someone else to be a major thing, but anything done in the name of love couldn't be questioned.

"Mr. Monroe?" A female asked, stepping into the room.

It was easy to see what she did for a living because everything I could see on her except for her face was covered in tattoos. She was still a cute blend, petite, but cute.

"That's me," I replied.

"My name is Elle and I'm one of the artists that you booked an appointment with. Rick will be coming momentarily. Which one of you am I working on?" she asked, looking back and forth between Katrina and I.

My wife's smile stayed firmly in place, but I could feel that chill coming from her again.

"Ladies first," I said, gesturing toward Katrina.

"Aw, thanks, bae," she said, reaching over and taking my hand.

And just like that the chill was gone. Elle got to work on her and couple minutes later, a Spanish guy named Big Rick got down to business on me.

I decided to get the initials K-A-T down my right forearm in big bold letters, but Katrina went even harder than that by getting my name and our wedding anniversary across her chest.

Two hours later, we both got out of our chairs and inspected each other's ink thoroughly.

"I love it," I said.

"Me, too," she replied, pulling me to her and kissing me with barely restrained hunger.

We elected not to get our tats wrapped after they were cleaned, wanting to show them off instead.

"You both did a phenomenal job," I said, pulling money out of my pocket and tipping them each and extra fifty dollars, on top of the agreed upon price.

Once we got back out-front, Katrina was heading for the door, but I stopped her by the front desk.

"Hold on a second, babe," I said, going to the receptionist and saying something to her. She nodded her head and picked up the phone. After everything was straight, I went to stand next to Katrina to wait on her next surprise.

"Is something wrong, Ahmani?"

"No, everything is just as it should be, but I have another surprise."

"What is it?" she asked excitedly.

Before I could answer, a young black woman approached us smiling.

"Everything come out okay, Mr. Monroe?"

"Indeed, it did, Jocelyn, is everything ready on your end?" I asked.

"Which one of you is gonna tell me what's going on?" Katrina asked.

"I apologize, Jocelyn, this is my wife, Katrina. Katrina this is the owner of this fine establishment," I replied.

"Well, I *was* the owner," Jocelyn said, smiling.

"Was? I don't understand," Katrina said confused.

"What she means is that *we're* now the new owners of Fryed Ink," I replied.

"You bought a tattoo shop?" Katrina asked in disbelief.

"No, baby, I bought a memory that we'll share for the rest of our lives," I said sincerely.

For a second, I thought she was gonna be mad, but then I saw the tears and the smile right before she leapt into my arms, and covered my face with kisses.

"I take it that you approve, which means we can leave now. Jocelyn send all the necessary paperwork to my lawyer and I'll be in touch," I said, carrying Katrina out into the afternoon sunlight.

"I'll do that. You two have a nice day," Jocelyn replied.

"Bae, I'm gonna have to put you down so I can drive," I said, once we got to the car.

"I want you to fuck me on the hood of the car, right here, right now," she demanded huskily.

"Sweetheart, we've got somewhere else to be, but I'll definitely cash that rain check."

I could feel the reluctance in every muscle of her body as she slowly uncoiled herself from me.

"I'll make it up to you. I promise," I said, kissing her quickly.

"Oh, I know you will, and it better be soon or I'm gonna take the dick."

44

Somehow, I knew her threat wasn't an idle one. We both got in the car and I pointed us in the direction of our next destination. Everything was all good until Katrina saw where we were.

"Why are you bringing me to Georgetown South, and don't even *think* about saying you bought a house out here," she said seriously.

"Relax, my love, we're just here for a cookout. I want you to know as much about me as I do myself, so I figured that I needed to bring you around the people who know me best."

She didn't say anything, but I could feel her unease as I pulled up in front of Amee's house.

There was an intimate gathering of about fifteen people, the grill was already fired up, and the music was bumping.

"I promise you're alright, baby, you're with me," I said, bringing her hand to my lips and kissing the back of it.

Once she nodded her head, we got out of the car. Up until that point, I hadn't noticed the swarm of police cars at the top of the hill, but now they were hard to miss.

"What's going on up there?" I asked Black Boy when he met us on the sidewalk.

"Oh, they found a decomposed body in a dumpster this morning," he replied.

The look Katrina turned on me said one word. *See*!

"It was probably a junky or something," I said.

"Nah, actually I heard that it was some dude not from around here," Black Boy replied.

"Oh, yeah?" I asked.

"Yeah, they found some I.D on him. Said his name was Robert Cook."

Aryanna

Chapter 5

If the gasp out of Katrina's mouth hadn't been so loud, I wouldn't have looked at her.

"You okay, babe?" I asked, taking her hand in my own again.

"I'm fine," she replied.

"That may be true, Mrs. Monroe, but there is the matter of that half a million dollars that we need to discuss," Black Boy said.

"Half a million dollars? What the fuck are *you* talking about?" I asked him, glad that I still had my gun on me.

"Easy, big fella, your wife can explain," he assured me.

When I turned my eyes back to Katrina, I could tell she was uneasy, but she wasn't scared or acting like she had some devastating secret to hide. She did look around to see if anyone was paying us any attention before she started speaking.

"When your family was killed, you asked me to put my money where my mouth was and offer a price for the name of the person responsible. We started out with one hundred thousand, but that wasn't doing it so I came to see Ira and added four hundred thousand more to it," she said calmly.

"You did that for me?" I asked, touched by her support and love.

"Yep, she did that. And I did what I do best," Black Boy stated, smiling.

"Which means that I owe you half a million. How would you like that, cashier's check or cash?" Katrina asked.

"Well if it's all the same to you, I'd rather not walk into a bank and ask for half a million dollars, not even with valid documentation proving that I'm entitled to do so," Black Boy replied.

"I understand. Bae, give me your gun," she said, holding her handout.

"My gun? Why?" I asked.

"Because I'm about to go pick up half a million dollars, and I damn sure don't want to ride around unarmed with all that on me. Give me your keys, too," she demanded.

After looking to make sure there were no cops in sight, I passed her both things she asked for.

"I'll be back shortly," she said, giving me a quick kiss before getting in the car and backing out.

"Have you always been so skilled at driving women away?" I asked, looking at Black Boy.

"Good to see that bullet ain't affect your sense of humor, nigga."

"I'm just sayin'. And why didn't you say something about the money this morning?" I asked.

"Because the deal wasn't made between you and me, it was made between me and her. That ain't no chump change, slim, so I needed to know she was gonna keep her word."

"Or?" I asked, feeling like an obvious threat was somehow implied.

His response to my question was a look that would've been easy to interpret whether I knew him or not.

"I don't know why everybody is so against my wife, but I brought her out here to get to know everyone who knows me. I ain't for the bullshit, though, so you might wanna make that clear to everybody," I said seriously.

I could see the evaluation in the way he was staring at me, but it didn't unsettle me or change what I'd said.

"You're different," he said neutrally.

"Wouldn't you be if you'd gone through what I have?"

"You're right but I saw the change in you before you got shot. I saw it the moment you pulled the trigger and scattered Robert Cook's thoughts all over the wall," he replied.

"What are you talking about?"

"As close as we are, you don't really think I'd take care of dude without you, do you? I got the info you wanted, but you ended him, bruh. Vengeance is yours, remember that," he said, before walking away and leaving me standing there.

I contemplated his words until I saw Amee standing in her doorway, signaling for me to come over. I quickly swiped a hotdog and a bun off the table, speaking to those who spoke to me, and made my way over to where Amee stood waiting.

"You want some of my hotdog," I offered.

"You so damn nasty!" she replied, laughing and pulling me inside.

"I was just trying to be a gentleman."

"Yeah, I'm sure you were. I can tell that your intentions were noble by the smirk on your face," she replied, hitting me playfully.

"Fine, I'll just eat it my damn self."

Before I could do that, though, she took it from me, bit it in half and gave it back.

"Dammmmnnn," I whispered.

"Oh, shut up! You acting like I didn't have way more meat than this in my mouth when you were here earlier."

I wanted to say something smart, but instead I chose to reflect on the memory of our time spent together in the wee hours of the morning. Even with her standing in front of me wearing jean shorts and a t-shirt, I could still see her naked body covered in out sweat, and then covered in soap.

"You were amazing," I said honestly.

"I know, but there's some things we need to get straight first of all, I ain't no hoe and I normally keep a lock on the pussy like it's a Brinks truck. I also don't fuck with married men or dudes in a relationship, and I *damn* sure don't let no one fuck me without a condom. It goes without saying that your black ass is the one-time exception to all of those rules, but you still need to hear what I'm saying."

"I hear you," I replied, finishing my hotdog.

"Good. Now secondly, if you let what happened this morning between us fuck up our lifelong friendship, I'ma kick your *motherfucking ass*! Understand?"

"Understood. I just have one question," I said, raising my hand like I was in school.

"What, boy?"

"Did you really say *one-time exception*? As in we won't be doing any of that again?" I asked.

"No, we won't because…"

I didn't let her finish the sentence before my mouth latched onto hers with a possessive hunger. I pushed her further into the house until we were almost in the living room. I could tell that I'd succeeded in overwhelming all of her senses, leaving her no option except to either kiss me back or drown in her own lust. The way her tongue moved with mine let it be known which path she'd taken. Before she could realize what was going on, I had her shorts around her ankles, my jeans around mine, and I'd spun her around until her soft ass cheeks were rubbing my dick.

"Bend over," I demanded, wrapping my hand up in her long, curly hair.

Her quick compliance earned her a feeding of dick, nice and slow, until no air could pass between us.

When I pulled back, I found out just how strong her pussy grip was because I was forced to dive immediately back inside of her. Even over the noise outside, I could hear the wetness from every splash I made in her ocean. With each stroke her pussy taunted me, forcing me to move faster and fuck her harder.

"I'ma cum!" She moaned right before her pussy spasmed violently.

Her declaration nor the act itself made me relent, I simply grabbed a stronger grip on her hair and tried to blow her back out.

"Hey, Amee, do you want a plate of—ohhh, nah, I think you're good," Black Boy said, opening and closing her front door just as quickly.

Not even that interruption made me break stride.

"Ah—Ahmani, we should, we should—Ssss."

I felt like I knew what she was trying to say, but the pounding I was giving her had the words stuck in her throat.

"Fuck!" she exclaimed loudly, announcing the arrival of her next orgasm.

"Oh, shit," I growled, cumming with her while praying I didn't collapse before I finished.

It was a long moment before I was able to let her hair go and gently unjointed our bodies.

"Let me help you out," I said, pulling her shorts back up for her, before doing the same with my jeans.

"You're an asshole, you know that," she stated, turning around to face me.

"What did I do?"

"You know what you did, nigga, and now so does Black Boy. You couldn't have taken me to my bedroom?" she asked.

I knew she wasn't really angry and the proof of that was she didn't resist when I pulled her toward me and kissed her again.

"You think you slick, don't you? Ahmani, I can't be your side bitch, you know I deserve better."

From what I knew about Amee, she wasn't side bitch material and I'd be a fool to try and turn her into one. It was something about her, though, that called to me that made every irrational decision I'd made with regards to her seem rational. The feelings she created in me made me believe that even if Katrina was perfect, Amee and I would still have this unshakeable chemistry.

"You're right, and I would never disrespect you by asking you to be my side bitch," I replied.

"You say that, but the look in your eyes says that you want to fuck me again right now."

"And the look in your eyes tells me you want the same thing," I stated seriously.

We stood there simply staring at each other for a few seconds, but then she took a step back, straightened her clothes, and walked out of the house. There was nothing in my mind that could explain the sexual connection and want I had for Amee, forcing me to believe it was something beyond any word description that had its hooks in me.

I didn't want to hurt her, though, so I had to learn to control myself and my desires. Physically, we may have wanted the same things, but emotionally we were at different places. I went to the bathroom and washed my dick, and then I made my way back to the cookout. I immediately spotted Amee making herself a plate of food, but I chose to keep my distance.

"My nigga, you *really* trying to make me kill you, ain't you?" Black Boy asked, walking over to me.

"Why you say that?"

"Because you *know* I can't let you hurt Amee, bruh. You would be telling me the same shit if I'd got caught fucking her," he said.

"I'm not gonna hurt her, don't worry."

"You better not, I'm just sayin'. Tell me the truth, though, was it…"

"You already know we ain't bout to have any type of conversation about what you walked in on," I said, cutting short whatever he was about to say.

Undoubtedly, he probably would've pressed the issue had it not been for Katrina pulling up. Seeing my Porsche had his mind focused on one thing. That almighty dollar.

"Come on," I said, leading the way to the car.

When my wife got out empty handed, I thought I was gonna have to shoot Black Boy for sure, but once we made it to her she popped the trunk and revealed a duffle bag.

"You wanna count it?" she asked.

Black Boy leaned down and unzipped the bag, moved some money around and zipped the bag back up.

"Nah, it looks like it's all there. Two hundred fifty thousand belongs to your husband, though, so if you'll kindly take that out, I'll handle the rest," Black Boy replied.

"Wait, why is two hundred fifty thousand Ahmani's?" she asked quickly.

"Let's just say he had a hand in helping ol' boy reach the afterlife," Black Boy said cryptically.

Katrina looked at me with more than a few questions in her eyes, but before I could respond, she made an executive decision.

"Take it all. Ahmani didn't have a hand in anything," she stated, giving both of us knowing looks.

"Whatever you say," Black Boy, replied, hoisting the bag up out of the trunk.

I thought he was gonna take it to his house, but instead he took it to the trunk of his Mustang and tossed it in. One thing I knew for certain was he had to believe he was a helluva nigga to just throw five hundred thousand in his trunk, and go back to the festivities like a muthafucka wouldn't kill his own momma for that type of bread.

"Bae, why didn't you tell me that you'd done that for me?" I asked, pulling her into my arms.

"Because I'd felt bad that nothing had come of it, but apparently I was wrong. Do I even wanna know what he meant when he said you had a hand in what happened?"

"No because it's not important. What's important is that that's behind us," I replied.

"Yeah, I just wish we could get rid of Aaron that easily. I mean, it's crazy that this muthafucka killed my parents but he's still alive."

We'd had more than one conversation about that before, especially with his trial coming up in the not so distant future.

"There's still time, bae," I said, hugging her to me and kissing her on the top of the head.

"Your baby like's barbecue because my stomach is growling," she proclaimed.

"Come on, let me feed you two before you get violent."

After we had plates of food in our hands, we made our way around and talked to a bunch of different people. Eventually, the crowd grew because the kids got let out of school, but that only increased the fun as the old heads told stories about me at that age.

It seemed like everybody was having a good time, even Katrina who was surrounded by the older women when they found out she was pregnant with the next generation. I even caught Amee laughing and joking, but somehow no matter where I was, she ended up on the opposite side of the party from me, and I knew that wasn't an accident.

Still, the day passed without drama and negativity, and that made it a success in my eyes because I knew Katrina had been expecting both.

By the time the streetlights came on, we were making our rounds and saying our goodbyes, when I finally found myself face to face with Amee. I pulled her into a hug and kissed her on the ear discreetly.

"I love you," I whispered.

"Then don't hurt me, Ahmani, I mean it."

"I promise," I replied, sucking her earlobe this time, before quickly letting her go.

The look Black Boy was giving me said I better keep that promise.

Hand in hand, Katrina and I walked to the car and once I'd helped her into her seat, I got behind the wheel.

"I hope you're not too tired, baby," she said.

"Why do you say that?"

"Oh, because I meant what I told you earlier. I'm getting some dick tonight, one way or another," she promised, smiling devilishly.

I could only laugh as I started the car and pulled off.

"Don't worry, sweetheart, I wouldn't *dream* of sending you to bed sexually frustrated. As a matter of fact…"

"Get the fuck out the car," a voice demanded calmly, sticking a gun to my head.

I had just pulled up to the four way stop, two blocks from all of my people and a nigga was really pulling a jack move on me.

"Listen, bruh, I don't…"

"Fuck that shit you talking, nigga, get out the goddamn car or I'ma splatter you all over your bitch," the jacker promised.

As soon as the thought crossed my mind about my pistol that Katrina had, I heard a deafening roar as the muzzle flashed inches from my face. The gun that was at my temple suddenly vanished along with the mufucka holding it, and I wasted no time mashing on the gas and speeding away. My run was short lived through because blue lights lit up the night behind me.

"Ahmani, pull over."

"What? Are you crazy?" I asked, looking at her sideways.

"Baby, if we run, we look guilty. Trust me, *pull over*."

Everything in me was screaming hell nah, but I had to trust that she knew what she was talking about.

"Bae, give me the gun, I…"

"No, Ahmani, I got this. I'm gonna tell them the truth."

Chapter 6
Two days later

"I don't mean to sound impatient, Mr. Sprano because I know first-hand that you're a miracle worker, but can you explain to me why my wife is still in jail?" I asked, taking a seat across from him at his desk.

"It's simple really, they're trying to decide whether or not to charge her with murder."

"Murder? That's some bullshit! That mufucka was trying to car jack us, and my wife defended us," I replied, angrily.

"You're right, but Virginia doesn't have a Stand Your Ground law, so Katrina has to go through the legal process."

"Okay, so once they officially charge her, will she get a bond?" I asked, hopeful.

"That's about a fifty/fifty chance, but I'm hoping the worst-case scenario is house arrest."

"When will we know for sure?" I asked.

"Well, the cops have to make a move today because it's been forty-eight hours, so I'll be in my office until I hear something."

"What am I supposed to do until, then? It's driving me crazy knowing that she has to go through this *and* she's pregnant," I said.

"You know better than anyone that these things take time, Ahmani, so all that you can really do is be patient."

It was on the tip of my tongue to tell this man exactly what I thought about being patient, but my ringing phone captivated my attention. I already knew it was Katrina before I got it out and put it to my ear, because she'd been calling me every hour on the hour since she'd got to the jail.

"Hey, baby, you okay?" I asked, as soon as we got through the automated system.

"I'm okay, I guess. Why didn't you tell me how bad the food was in this place?"

"Trust me that's something I'm glad to forget, and never did I expect you to be in that situation, sweetheart," I replied.

"Yeah, me either. Have you talked to my lawyer?"

"I'm actually sitting in his office right now, pressing him about getting you out," I said.

"Tell him that I don't care *what* the bond amount is, he better get me out the same day. You have access to everything, Ahmani, so I'm expecting you to do whatever is necessary."

"Bae, that goes without saying. I'll go to the bank and pull out all the cash that you tell me to right now if you want," I offered.

"I just want you to be ready because I wanna come *home*. I don't like it in here."

I hated the sadness and depression that had filled her voice.

"Have you been seen by a doctor yet?" I asked.

"I'm supposed to see one sometime today, as long as it's a woman. No man's hands will ever touch me except yours."

"We've got some news," Mr. Sprano said, looking at his computer screen.

"Hold on, babe, I'm 'bout to put you on speaker phone," I said.

"Katrina, can you hear me?" Mr. Sprano asked.

"Yeah, I can hear you."

"Okay, I just got word that you're gonna be charged with manslaughter and the plea…"

"I'm not taking a plea," she stated quickly.

The look the lawyer gave me said he didn't necessarily agree with the position Katrina was taking, but that was a fight for later.

"My focus right now is on getting you a reasonable bond, so I'm going to handle that and I'm hoping they formally charge you in the next few hours so I can get you out today," Mr Sprano said.

"That sounds like a plan," she replied, sounding somewhat relieved.

"Call me when the plan comes together," I said, taking the call off speaker phone as I stood up to leave.

I shook hands with the lawyer and then left his office.

"So, baby, what's the first thing you wanna eat when you get out?" I asked.

"I don't care, but I want it to be something that you cook."

"Oh, yeah? You miss my cooking like that?" I asked smiling.

"Yeah. Plus, I don't want to go out because as soon as I finish eating my food I'ma eat that dick for dessert."

Despite my laughter, I knew she was serious. Since she'd been locked up, she'd told me stories about how she used to play with her pussy on the phone for me. Of course, those conversations always led to me having to get the grease, pull my stick out, and make that thang pop over the phone. It's amazing what we'd do for the people we loved.

"It's been too long since I explored the back of your throat with this big mufucka, so I'm definitely looking forward to that. I'll agree to feed you first, though, so what do you want me to cook for you?"

"Surprise me," she replied.

"I can always do that," I said, climbing behind the wheel.

"Where are you about to go now?"

"Well, I don't see any point in going all the way home when you could be out in a matter of hours, so I guess I'll go grocery shopping," I reasoned.

"Babe, you can't just be riding around with meat in your car, I don't want food poisoning my first day out."

"I feel that. Why don't I cook for you tomorrow then and we can just grab a quick bite on the way home," I suggested.

"I'm okay with that, but that brings me back to my original question. Where are you about to go now?"

"I. Don't know," I replied slowly, getting a feeling about where this conversation was about to go. When I suddenly heard her name called in the background, I breathed a sigh of relief because I was saved by the bell.

"I've gotta go to the medical department to see the doctor, but I'll call you when I come back," she said.

"A'ight, bae, I love you."

"If you love me, Ahmani, then stay out of Georgetown South," she replied, disconnecting our call.

I shook my head and chuckled as I put my phone down, started the car, and pulled off.

Fifteen minutes later, I pulled up right next to Black Boy's Mustang and hopped out.

"I hope this is important," I said, looking at him leaning against his ride.

"Yeah, it is. I need a favor."

"Maybe I should rephrase, I hope this is important *to me*," I stated.

"Come on, my nigga, you know that the code of the streets is a favor for a favor. I wouldn't be asking you for one unless I was prepared to give up one or more in return."

The statement of *or more* that he'd made was enough to pique my interest.

"I'm listening," I said.

"So, I got that half a mill from your old lady, right? But a street nigga with that type of money and no legal avenues to spend it is asking to go to the Feds. I could buy cars, jewelry, and that other dumb shit, but I ain't on that. Sure, I could spend it slowly, but tomorrow ain't promised to no one, *especially* not a nigga like me. So, what I'm saying is that I need you to help me spend this money."

"What are you trying to buy?" I asked curiously.

"I wanna get Amee and Isaiah a house, move them out the hood."

His statement was like a well-placed punch to the chin, revealing to me how selfish my own action had been. Between the two of us I was the nigga fucking her, but he was the one willing to really take care of her, and that made it clear the type of piece of shit I was.

"What about you? You gonna move out the hood?" I asked.

My question caused him to look up and down the streets that he considered his, and I could tell he was contemplating heavily.

"Believe it or not, I actually think I'm ready to move. I mean the south will respect me whether I live here or not, but if all the shit that I've done ain't about building a better life then what did I do it for?"

"I can feel that. So, where do you want these houses to be?" I asked.

"You can talk to Amee about hers, but I ain't going too far. I'll let you know when I find something. In the meantime, I'ma give you this, though," he said, going to his trunk and coming back with the same duffle bag that Katrina had given him a couple days ago.

"You trust me with half a million dollars?"

"More than I do with her," he replied, nodding up the sidewalk.

I turned to find Amee headed in our direction.

"I got some moves to make, but don't forget what I said," he warned, giving me a pound before climbing in his car and pulling off.

"What's up, Trouble?" Amee asked, stopping in front of my car.

"Me? Trouble?"

"Yeah you, nigga, everywhere you go trouble just seems to follow your ass," she said, shaking her head.

"That shit don't even be my fault sometimes, I mean, I didn't tell dude to try and get me for my ride."

"I guess you're right *this* time, and from what I hear your girl is a helluva shot. Hit ol' boy right between the eyes," she said, looking at me in a weird way.

"That was damn sure better than ol' boy shooting me because I know damn well I couldn't survive two head shots in one lifetime."

I'd meant my comment to be funny, but I could tell she thought it was anything but that, so I moved on.

"Let me ask you something, Amee, if you could live anywhere, where would it be?"

"Some place where its warm all the time," she answered quickly.

I had figured as much because during our early morning conversations, she'd told me about her Reflex Sympathetic Dystrophy syndrome, and the constant pain she was in because of it. I wished the money at my feet could buy her a cure, but as of yet one didn't exist, so she had to suffer in silence.

"So, is this warm place in the United States or we're you thinking some place foreign?"

"Why? Are you gonna buy me an island, or half of Brazil?" she asked sarcastically.

Being that she was already standing by the front of the car I just picked the duffle bag up, and carried it to the trunk.

"Let me show you something," I said, opening the trunk and sitting the bag inside.

Once I had her undivided attention, I opened the bag to reveal the bundles of cash.

"Boy, what the fuck are you doing with that kind of money out here?" she asked in a panicked whisper, looking around like the goons could smell money wherever they were at.

"Calm down, I just picked it up from Black Boy so that I can do something for him,"

"Something like what, Ahmani? That's a lot of fucking money," she stated, looking in the bag again.

"Come on, let's go get something to eat and I'll explain," I replied, zipping the bag closed and closing the trunk.

I saw the hesitation clearly in her eyes, but she still climbed in the passenger side.

"Go get something to eat better not be code for park somewhere and fuck either, nigga."

"Girl, please, you got way too much ass for me to be trying anything in this little ass car," I replied, laughing as I slid behind the wheel and got us on the move.

"Fuck you!"

"Didn't you just say we weren't doing that," I said, flashing her a mischievous smile.

This time she hit me instead of saying anything, but that only made me laugh again.

Our conversation was just regular small talk until we were sitting in the parking lot of Sonic with our food.

"Alright, so, I'ma keep it real with you, Amee. Black Boy and I ain't on no dumb shit, he's just smart enough to know that he can't spend that type of money without attracting attention. I can help with that."

"Is that it? You could've told me all this without having to buy me lunch," she replied.

"Like your ass had something to do at two o'clock in the afternoon. Oh, there's more. The first thing he wants me to buy is a house for you and Isaiah, out of the hood and wherever you wanna go."

He said that? Really?" she asked emotionally.

"Yeah, he did. I'm only sorry that I didn't think of it first."

For a moment, she was at a loss for words, and her food was forgotten as she looked out the windshield with tears sliding down her face.

"He would do some over-the-top shit like that, and of course, it would be you who helps him. I can't accept that though, I can't…"

"You can and you will because you know that neither of us is taking no for an answer. You deserve something good in life sweetheart, and I know that you want better for Isaiah. This is your chance," I said, taking her hand in mine.

The tears began cascading down her beautiful face, but she finally nodded her head in acceptance. Despite my earlier vow to myself about resisting the temptation to dance in the fire that existed between us, I still leaned toward her until our lips touched. The temperature was just beginning to heat up when my ringing phone interrupted us. I knew who it was so I knew answering was mandatory.

"Hey, baby," I said, never taking my eyes off of Amee.

"I've got two surprises for you, my love," Katrina said, with obvious joy in her voice.

"Oh, yeah, what are they?"

"Come get me and I'll show you," she promised.

"You got a bond already?" I asked surprised.

"It's two hundred thousand dollars, but yeah I got one. How long will it take you to get here?"

"I'm on my way now," I replied, starting the car and putting it into gear.

"I'll be waiting. I love you, bae."

"Love you, too," I said, hanging up.

"So, your wife is getting out, huh?" Amee asked.

"Yeah finally. Jail ain't no place for a pregnant woman."

"You ain't lying about that. How much did Black Boy say to spend on a house for me and Isaiah?" she asked.

"You get whatever you want, wherever you want. I'll cover whatever the extra is."

"Ahmani, you don't have to…"

"Stop talking and finish your food," I said, pulling off.

It didn't take long for me to get us back to Georgetown South, but when I pulled up, things had gone from sugar to shit.

"Oh, God," Amee said under her breath, taking the words right out of my mouth.

In front of us were three cop cars, six cops and Black Boy face down on the hood of his Mustang with handcuffs on. On the roof of his car sat his infamous AK-47 and a pistol, which spelled trouble in every language.

"Amee, you gotta find out what's going on, and then call me *a.s.a.p.*! I'll do everything I can to get him out," I vowed.

"Okay," she replied hurriedly getting out of the car.

Black Boy and I locked eyes, and I nodded at him to let him know I had his back. The nigga actually had the audacity to smile, which made me smile as I backed up and turned my car around.

I drove slow out of the neighborhood, but once I got on route 223, I let my car eat up the road in an effort to get to the jail as fast as I could.

When I got there twenty minutes later, I had a decision to make. I had no doubt that I could get a bondsman to go get

Katrina out, but I didn't want her spending a moment longer than necessary inside that raggedy mufucka. So, I took three hundred thousand dollars out of the duffle bag and strolled inside Prince William county jail on some boss shit.

"I'm here to post bond for my wife, Katrina Monroe," I said, to the cop behind the glass.

"Cash or are you using a bondsman?"

"Cash," I replied.

A few key strokes later the female looks up at me with a smirk on her face.

"It says here that your wife's bond is two hundred thousand dollars, you got that in cash?" she asked.

I opened the duffle bag and pulled out the two square bundles wrapped in plastic, sitting them right in the window for her to see.

An hour and a half later, Katrina walked out and hopped straight into my arms.

"I missed you so much, baby," she said, kissing me passionately.

I carried her out front and to the car, barely able to see because somehow my tongue kept ending up in a furious battle with hers.

"Babe, you gotta get down so that you can get in the car," I said, laughing.

After several more kisses, she let go of me long enough for us to get in the car, but she had my dick free of my jeans before I could get the key in the ignition.

"I know you wanna give me my surprises, but we need to wait," I told her.

"Oh, this isn't a surprise, you already *knew* you was giving up this dick. Here's your surprise," she said, reaching in her bra and pulling out a piece of paper.

I opened it, but I didn't see it because she had my dick in her mouth and my brain lost the ability to concentrate. Somehow, I managed to fight through and I realized that I was looking at a sonogram picture.

"We're having a girl," I stammered.

"Look closer," she said, before diving head first back on my now throbbing dick. I did like she told me, but when I realized what I was seeing I grabbed a fistful of her hair and pulled her up to my eye level.

"Baby, am I looking at this right?" I asked.

"Yep. We're having twins."

Aryanna

Chapter 7

"You're fucking with me, right?" I asked, stunned.

"Why would I do that? And where in the hell would I be able to get a fake sonogram picture in jail?"

My eyes immediately went back to the picture I was now clutching with a death grip, and sure enough her name was printed in the bottom left corner.

"Baby, you're five months pregnant and you've had multiple doctors' appointments, so how the fuck had the doctor not see this before now?" I asked, trying to fight through my shock, and make sense out of this.

"I asked the same thing, and the doctor inside told me that it's not uncommon for one baby to hide behind another for a while before making a sudden appearance."

"Oh, it was sudden, alright," I mumbled.

"Either way, we now are expecting two healthy baby girls in a few months, and I'm probably gonna have a C-section, so they don't tear the lining out of my pussy. Now will you please either let my hair go or loosen your grip so I can finish what I started."

I let her go, but I put my dick away because head was the last thing on my mind.

"Hey, I wasn't done with that," she complained.

"Later," I replied, starting the car and pulling off.

She sat back in the seat with a serious pout on her face, but all I could think about was the picture still in my hand.

"If I didn't know any better, Ahmani, I'd think you weren't excited about us having twins."

"Of course, I'm excited, baby, I'm just surprised right now," I said quickly.

"Too surprised to get your dick sucked? Or is somebody else doing that for you now?" she asked, her tone heavy with accusation.

My mind immediately went to Amee and the soft lips I'd just felt on my own earlier, but there was no way that would be my response to my wife.

"Why would you even say some shit like that, Katrina? You got a guilty conscience or something? Was you in there sucking dick for favors?"

"You know I would *never* cheat on you..."

"Oh, but since I did in the past that means that I will again?" I asked, going on the defensive.

"So, you can put words in my mouth, but not your dick, right? I never brought up your past, *you* did. And what the fuck are we arguing about anyway, most muthafuckas would be *happy* to let their wife suck their dick!"

"You wanna suck my dick?" I asked, tucking the sonogram picture into my pocket.

When she didn't respond verbally, I decided to take matters into my own hands.

"I can't hear you," I said, pulling my dick back out and grabbing her roughly by the hair.

When I pushed her head into my lap, she took me into her mouth without hesitation, but I made sure she gagged by pushing that mufucka to the back of her throat mercilessly.

"That's right, suck this dick, bitch," I said, steadily tightening the grip I had on her hair, as I merged onto the highway.

I could tell she liked my rough treatment of her because she was devouring me with a fat girl's enthusiasm.

Before I knew it, the speedometer on the car was saying I was doing a 150 m.p.h., but I kept my foot on the gas while weaving through traffic. I could feel my toes wanting to curl, but I fought against my climax because I wanted to make her earn it.

Her lips were so soft and moist, and her mouth just got wetter the longer she kept me locked within her strong jaws. When she suddenly started humming with the same power of the engine's vibration, the fight was over and my cum rocketed down her throat.

She swallowed every drop like I knew she would, but then she thought it was over.

"Now suck it until its hard again," I demanded, pushing her head right back down when she tried to pull my dick completely out of her mouth.

She tried to say something, but it was coming out as nothing except mumbles. Before I knew it, she had me rock hard again, but this time I controlled the speed of how fast she got to gobble the dick.

Twenty minutes later, I was still throbbing under her expert technique when our exit came swiftly into view. I finally pulled her head from my lap, so I could fully concentrate on the exit ramp I was now taking at 100 m.p.h. I somehow managed not to leave any paint on the guard rails, but we slid to a stop in a cloud of smoke and screaming tires, inches away from tapping another cars bumper. When I looked over at Katrina, her face was flushed red and her blue eyes were dancing with excitement.

"You still wanna get something to eat?" I asked, casually.

"Just take me home and fuck me."

"We'll get to that, but you're now eating for three so I definitely need to feed your hungry ass," I said.

"Okay, then, take me wherever. Just hurry, please."

I could hear the need in her voice with every word spoken, making me smile inwardly because it was understood who was in control. I pointed us in the direction of a nearby barbecue spot since I had the taste for some ribs my damn self.

"Baby, couldn't we just hit a drive-through?" she asked, clearly growing more sexually frustrated by the minute.

"The food here is good, and it won't take long. Sit there and look pretty," I said, fixing my clothing before I stepped out to go inside the restaurant.

Within a couple minutes, I had our orders placed and I was headed back to the car to wait. The expression on her face through the windshield gave me the perfect idea of how to kill some time.

"Our food will be ready in about fifteen to twenty minutes," I informed her, standing at her door.

As I'd expected, her frown got deeper and the lines on her forehead became more pronounced, but that only made me smile.

"Come here and let me talk to you," I said, opening her door.

She took the hand I offered and climbed out of the car, intentionally opening her legs so I could see that she'd removed her panties from under her Gucci dress.

In fact, she'd put them on the steering wheel, making her desires clear. As I led her to the front of the car, I scanned the parking lot, noticing that it was barely full, even though darkness was settling around us.

I knew there would probably be families coming out to enjoy a good meal once it got dark, which meant there wasn't a lot of time to waste.

My first kiss was soft, sensual even, but I conveyed hunger and hers matched me in spirit. I had no doubt that she figured we were about to engage in a heavy make out session when I leaned her back on the hood of the car, but the moment I opened her legs and pushed my dick inside of her, she knew what my intentions were. was.

"Baby, people will see us," she panted, locking her legs around my waist.

"Let them see," I whispered, bringing my face inches from hers while delivering stroke after pounding stroke.

She tried kissing me again, but I wasn't about to muffle her sounds of pleasure.

"Whose dick is this?" I asked.

"Mine!"

"*Whose-dick-is-this*?" I growled, fucking her harder with each word spoken.

"It's—It's mine! All mine!" She screamed, damn near delirious as her first orgasm rocked her.

It wasn't a conscious thought for me to choke her, but when my hand suddenly gripped her throat, I went with it. The harder I squeezed the more her body reacted, and I almost lost myself down the rabbit hole of climax before I was ready. I could feel her sanity getting ready to come apart again under the pressure of the blows I was giving her, but I stopped before it got that far.

"Bae..."

"Shut up," I said, standing up and roughly flipping her over.

Her dress flew up her back, leaving me with a beautiful view of her succulent ass cheeks. It had been my intention to simply suck her from the back, but when I saw the trail of her pussy juices and cum running down the hood of the car, I knew I had enough lubrication to have all of her.

"Spread your ass cheeks," I demanded.

She complied without hesitation, putting her face and neck on the hood of the car as quickly as she would our bedroom pillow. I gave the illusion of taking my time by easing the head of my dick in, but once I had a hold of her hips, I slammed every inch inside her like I was trying to plow through her.

"Ahmani!" she shrieked, immediately letting go of her ass cheeks in order to brace herself.

"Bitch, I said *shut-up*!" I growled through gritted teeth, fucking her with the same speed and power as I had when I was in her pussy.

Her moans and the sound of our skin slapping echoed across the parking lot loud enough to have me worried about the cops being called, but still I didn't stop. Right before I was about to cum, I pulled out of her ass and dove back inside the pussy, sending us both to another world.

"You good?" I asked, breathlessly, pulling her dress back down as I helped her up off the car.

"Better. Better than ever!" she replied, grinning from ear to ear.

"Good. I'm glad we could have this conversation."

"Uh huh, the definition of good talk," she said, tucking my dick back inside of my jeans for me.

I gave her a quick kiss before turning around and heading back to the restaurant to get our food. As soon as I walked in the door, I could tell by some of the stares aimed in my direction that quite a few people inside had caught the show and some even had their phones out making it obvious that they were recording us. I acted like nothing happened, though, and made my way to the pick-up counter. Before I could say anything, the cute red-head who'd taken my order was passing me my food, and a tiny piece of paper.

"Call me," she whispered, winking at me so it would be impossible to misunderstand what she was saying.

I tucked her number, grabbed my food, and headed toward the door. Before I could walk out, a thunderous applause started and that made me laugh as I headed back to the car.

"What was all that noise?" Katrina asked, accepting the bag of food and climbing back in the passenger seat.

"Our fans."

This statement made her blush, but I knew she had no regrets.

"What's gotten into you, Ahmani?

"What do you mean?" I asked, staring the car and guiding us home.

"I mean our sex life has *always* been amazing, but you're taking me to levels I ain't never experienced. I've never let a man talk to me like you do, or handle me like you do. I'd always thought that if you came out of your mouth and called me a bitch then I was gonna have to get ignorant, but baby I *wanna be* your bitch. I'll be your bitch, your whore, and everything in between, just as long as I'm your only one."

"You'll always be my only one, bae, you ain't never gotta worry about that," I said honestly.

"I'm sorry I reacted the way I did earlier."

"No, you're not because it got you fucked just the way that you wanted," I replied chuckling.

She didn't even try to put up an argument, but instead laughed right along with me because she knew that I was speaking the truth. With her sexual appetite sated for the moment she turned her attention on the delicious smelling food sitting in her lap.

"Don't eat my food," I said seriously.

She flashed her most mischievous smile at me before opening the lid on the first Styrofoam container and filling the car with the sweet scent of barbecue sauce.

"Now, baby, you know what's mine is yours and what yours is mine, so there's no way for me to eat your food," she said, picking up a boneless rib, and making it disappear in two bites.

"You can talk your ass off, but just stick to that container that you're eating and we won't have any problems wife."

She acted like she was too engrossed in her ribs, french fries, and biscuits to hear me, but if she knew like I knew she wouldn't play no games. Luckily, it only took ten minutes to get us home, and we set up shop in the kitchen immediately. It was amazing to me how after smashing a whole rack of ribs, fries, and three biscuits she could still be hungry, but before I could say anything, she was on the phone getting pizza. My ringing phone took my attention off of her, and put it on the person calling me.

"What up, light skin? Hello?" I said, when all I heard was silence.

"I'm here, you just caught me off guard because you use to call me light skin or little Amee all the time. For a second you sounded like the old Ahmani."

"You make it sounds like you don't like the new me," I said, acting like I was insulted.

"Boy, shut up, you know that's not what I meant. I love your crazy ass regardless and you know it."

"Yeah, I do. So, tell me what up, Little Amee?"

"What's up is they got Black Boy locked up on gun charges, but for some reason he's on a no bond hold," she replied.

Hearing that made no sense because if Katrina could get a bond for manslaughter, then surely Black Boy could get one for some guns.

"Something ain't right about that," I stated.

"I'm feeling the same way, but there's nothing that I can do about it."

"No, but I can. I'll get on top of it and I'll call you when I know something. If bruh calls you tell him to call me," I said.

"Okay. Thanks for lunch by the way, I owe you."

Hearing that made me smile, but I quickly toned it down because I felt Katrina's eyes on me.

"You're welcome. I'll holla at you later," I said, hanging up.

"Who was that?" Katrina asked, before I could put my phone away.

"Amee."

"Amee? And what did Amee have to say?" she asked.

"She just wanted me to know that Black Boy was locked up, but he doesn't have a bond."

"Are you really surprised by that, I mean you know the type of dude Ira is," she said.

"Yeah, I do, and that's why I told her that I would take care of it," I replied.

"Take care of it? How? Why? Why are you about to make *his* problems *our* problems?"

"Because like you said I know what type of dude Black Boy is, and I don't feel like his loyalty could ever be in question. I may not remember everything, but I don't think that he's the type to leave me in a fucked-up situation," I replied honestly.

"Really? Well if my memory serves me correctly, *I* was the one there for you while you were locked up last time, and you never mentioned Ira doing a damn thing for you."

"But we both know he did a lot for me when I got out, didn't he?" I asked, looking pointedly at her.

The truth stopped her from responding right away, but I knew it wouldn't be enough to take the fight out of her.

"Do you have a problem with my friendship with Black Boy and Amee?" I asked directly.

"I have a problem with you getting sucked back into your old life, Ahmani. You're about to be a father of *three* and that needs to be your focus because I'd hate for my kids to grow up without their father."

It was weird to me how that statement sounded more like a threat than something she'd regret. Before I could say anything, my phone started ringing again, and I answered. Her eyes bore into mine with the intensity of a police detective, but that didn't shake me or stop me from listening to the automated jail recording playing in my ear. I pressed one without hesitation.

"What's up, bruh?" I asked.

"A lot my nigga. I need to see you a.s.a.p.," Black Boy said.

"I got you, I'll have money on your commissary first thing tomorrow."

"I see you playing shit smart, and that's a good thing because we can't trust no one right now, especially not your wife," he stated.

"Yeah, I feel you. I'll tell her that you said hello, my nigga."

Chapter 8

The sun had barely risen, but I was already looking at the most beautiful sight my eyes had ever seen. In my arms was my son, drinking peacefully from his bottle while trying to fight off the next wave of sleep that was destined to claim him. I could see my features all over his little face, but he was undoubtedly Elyse's son because he'd inherited her gray eyes.

"You gonna get a lot of pussy because of those eyes," I whispered to him.

I knew he had absolutely no understanding of what I was saying, but the sound of my voice always made him smile. That warmed my heart, especially because I couldn't remember the sound of something as simple as my own father's voice.

My son nor my daughters would ever have to worry about that because come hell or high water, they would hear my voice everyday of their lives.

I was still trying to wrap my mind around the fact that Katrina was pregnant with twins, but I wasn't as panicked as I'd been yesterday. I had a firm idea in my mind about what kind of father I wanted to be, but more and more I was asking myself if that lined up with the mother Katrina was gonna be.

I wanted to instill basic values into all my kids, and the important of loyalty was a big one. My wife wanted me to forget the mud I'd come from just because I had a better life now, but she didn't understand that a slave who'd worked in the field wouldn't forget the blood, sweat, and tears.

It didn't matter if he moved to the big house because that slave would remember every lash he took, and who gave them. My loyalty could never be brought into question, so the decision I had to make wasn't a surprise to anyone. I'd been smart enough not to try and convince Katrina to see shit from my point of view because that would be a waste of time, and a senseless argument.

Instead, I'd pampered her with more food and more loving until she'd passed out from exhaustion. I'd thought I'd be able to find sleep, too, but the mystery that is my wife had made that impossible. It was seeming like every time that I thought I had her figured out she'd show me a different side of herself.

Just a few short days ago, she was handing Black Boy a half a million dollars in cold hard cash, and now she didn't want me to get involved in his life? For the first time, I was wondering if she was bi-polar. The only thing I knew for sure was that making her my wife didn't erase my past or rewrite history, and if she expected me to act like that, she was in for a surprise.

Turning my mind back to my son, I watched him empty his bottle just as sleep finally won the hard-fought battle. I watched him for a few more moments before kissing his tiny face, and putting him back in his crib. I made a quiet exit from his room and went back to mine with the intention of getting dressed, but I was met with a surprise.

"Katrina, why are you crying?"

Her hand immediately went to her face and I could tell that she was surprised to find wetness coating her finger tips.

"I don't know. I just woke up."

Climbing into bed beside her, I pulled her into my arms and held her.

"Did you have a nightmare?" I asked softly.

"I can't remember. I just feel sad for some reason that I can't really explain."

"Is there anything that I can do?" I asked.

She didn't say anything, she simply snuggled deeper into my arms. I laced my arms through hers so I could put both of my hands on her stomach and we stayed like that until long after the sun had laid it's claim to the sky.

"Are you hungry?" I asked.

"Only if you're gonna cook for me likes you promised."

"I think that I can do that," I replied, kissing her on the top of her head before unfolding myself from around her.

When I went to get out of bed, she grabbed my hand, lacing our fingers together to make it clear that she wasn't letting go, and forcing me to pull her behind me. When we got downstairs, I expected her to take a seat at the counter like she so often did to watch me cook, but she actually released my hand and went to the basement.

A few seconds later, I heard the muffled sounds of gunfire. By the time I'd finished making the pancakes and moved on to the sausage and eggs, she'd made the transition from a pistol to something fully automatic. I was beginning to question whether or not she'd truly forgotten whatever dream that had reduced her to tears because she was definitely exercising some demons. I'd thought that I was gonna have to go downstairs and pry the gun out of her hands, but by the time I had the food on the plates she'd found her way back upstairs.

"Of course, you show up after all the hard work is done," I said, sitting her food in front of her.

"I'm always with you in spirit, don't forget that."

"Sure, you are. Do you want to talk about whatever is on your mind?" I asked, taking a seat beside her with my own plate.

"I'm fine, bae, I was just a little tense that's all."

"Damn, my dick game must be falling off if you were tense after the workout, I gave you until the early morning hours," I said smiling.

"Very funny. Just so you know my eye still burns and my vision is slightly blurry from where you came in my eye," she replied, punching me in the arm.

"Babe, did you or did you not say cum on your face?"

"On my *face,* Ahmani, not directly in my eye!"

"You didn't see me cumming?" I asked, laughing hard at the expression on her face.

"You're an asshole, you know that? You're lucky I love you."

"Awww, bae, you act like you didn't cum all over my face *multiple* times last night," I said, stealing a sausage link off her plate.

"Boy, if you do that again I'm going back downstairs and get a gun to shoot your ass."

I quickly put my hands up in surrender and I didn't even flinch when she snatched a pancake off of my plate.

"So, what are you gonna do today?" she asked casually. A little too casually.

"I don't know, why do you have something in mind?"

"Not really, but I was thinking about what you said last night. You know about you and Black Boy," she said.

"Were you now? That's surprising."

"Ahmani, I *am* capable of admitting when I'm wrong, or when I've overreacted to a situation, once I've had time to look at everything."

"Uh huh. Well I can appreciate that, baby, it means a lot to me," I replied.

The passing seconds were filled by us eating our food in silence, but I was just waiting on the other shoe to hit the ground.

"I think that you should go see him," Katrina said suddenly.

The pancake that I was chewing on hid my smile, and it took a lot of effort not to laugh out loud.

"Go see him? Why do you think that I should do that?"

"Because it's not safe to talk on the phone, and I want you to make him another proposition. I want you to tell him we'll give him five hundred thousand dollars to take care of Aaron once and for all," she stated calmly.

I'd been wondering how long it was gonna take her to formulate this plan in her mind, but I'd known last night that she'd been too fired up to think clearly. It seemed that the fog had lifted.

"I can do that if you want me to."

"You know that I want you to, I want that shit *over* already," she replied passionately.

"Alright, calm down. I'll go see him today."

"I'd rather you do it while I'm still early because I want your undivided attention. I don't think that you realize just how much I missed you," she said, leaning over to kiss me.

I paused in my eating to indulge in the sweetness of her lips, loving how her epiphany was gonna work out for the both of us.

"Can you finish this for me?" I asked, pointing at my half full plate.

Without a word she swiped it and was hovering over it like she was eating in a prison chow hall. I laughed about that all the way upstairs and into the shower.

It only took me half an hour to wash last night's sex off me, get dressed, and get on the road. I sent Amee a text and told her to be ready because I was coming to get her so she could go to the jail with me because I knew a mufucka on the inside could never have too much morale support. In all actuality I was bringing Amee along to support me too because I had no idea what Black Boy was gonna tell me, but I had little doubt about whether or not I'd like it. When I pulled up in front of Amee's house, she wasn't outside waiting which caused me to blow my horn.

"Damn, you're impatient," she said, climbing into the passenger seat a few minutes later.

"I did text you and let you know I was coming, right?"

"Okay and I had to take a shower, I wasn't about to come out the house, funky nigga," she replied.

"Hot date last night?" I asked, speeding off.

"Actually, yeah."

I looked over at her to see if she was joking, but it appeared that she wasn't, nor was she gonna elaborate. I knew the feeling of anger that was building in me was one hundred percent irrational, but I couldn't do shit about it.

"You know you just ran a red light, right?" she asked.

My response was to push down harder on the gas pedal, which made her laugh.

"You think you're cute don't you, Amee?"

"Oh, I know I'm fine, but I think it's funny that your jealous, like you have some right to be," she replied, still snickering.

"I ain't jealous. I just remember this whole speech you gave me at the cookout about how you keep the pussy locked up tighter than a Brinks truck."

"And I most definitely do, so don't say nothing that's gonna get you cussed out," she warned.

I knew that taking her advice was my best bet so I continued driving and didn't say shit else. Before long we were pulling up in front of the jail.

"And just to be clear my hot date was with my son, we went and played laser tag," she said, opening the door to step out of the car.

"I'm sorry," I said, grabbing her wrist to stop her movement.

"Do you remember what else I told you the day of the cookout? I said that you better not let us fucking fuck up our friendship. Do I care about you? Yes? But I'm not yours, Ahmani, and you're not mine. Let's not bullshit each other," she replied, pulling free of my hold, and stepping out of the car.

Feeling sufficiently chastised, I got out the car and followed her inside. We had to wait damn near forty-five minutes to actually make it to the visiting area, and that time had passed in an awkward silence. Thankfully, it didn't take Black Boy long to get there.

"I hate seeing you like this," Amee said, picking up the phone first.

"Shit, I'm surprised you came to see me, I *know* you don't do jail visits," he replied.

"Yeah, well, I didn't exactly have a choice," Amee said, nodding toward me.

They talked for about ten minutes before she moved to the side and passed me the phone.

"What's good?" I asked.

"Shit, right now it's looking all bad bruh. The gun charges are the least of my worries."

"What else is there?" I asked.

"When they got me to the police station, they started asking me about dude they found in the neighborhood from out of town, and they weren't insinuating, they were talking like it was a *fact* it was me."

"Fishing probably," I said.

"You know that I know the difference. This sounded like somebody made an official statement that carries some weight, my nigga."

"And you think, what? That my wife did?" I asked skeptically.

"What I'm saying is that it ain't hard to separate fact from fiction when only certain people know the facts, feel me?"

I understood exactly what he was saying, but that still seemed like a stretch of the imagination, or a case of paranoia.

"I mean, I'll look into it, but I just don't know because we had a talk a couple hours ago about the same five hundred you gave me yesterday for that other nigga upstairs," I replied.

"Nah, I'm cool. I need to focus on what's going on right now, and I'ma need a helluva lawyer to do that."

"Say no more, it'll be taken care of today," I vowed.

"There's one more thing that I need you to do for me my nigga. I need you to get Amee and Isaiah out of town a.s.a.p."

"Hold up, why I gotta leave when…"

"Because I said so," Black Boy replied, giving her a look to silence her protests.

"I don't understand, bruh, why the move?" I asked, not liking the idea of Amee being far away.

"Because aside from me, Amee is the closest person to you, and for whatever reason the people close to you seem to have bad luck," he replied seriously.

It wasn't easy to digest what he was implying, but I had to ask myself how I would feel if Amee and Isaiah met with the same fate as my family had. I couldn't bear the thought of any more losses.

"I'll get it done, even if I gotta tie her ass up and throw her in the trunk," I said.

"I'll kick your ass if you try," Amee said quickly.

"I'm trusting you to handle that Ahmani. We family, you hear me?" Black Boy asked.

"I got you, that's my word. How much money do you want on your books?" I asked.

"A couple hundred should be good for now. Make sure you give Amee some money, and you know what to do with the rest," he replied.

"A'ight. Call me when you want me to come back up here," I said, standing up.

He nodded his head before putting his hand to the glass for me and Amee to touch. I could see the tears in her eyes, but she didn't let them fall until Black Boy had disappeared.

"Come on," I said, putting my arm around her shoulders and leading her the way we'd come. The walk back to my car was a long one, and my mind was racing trying to figure out the order of operations for everything that needed to happen. The first thing I did was use my phone to put money on Black Boys account through the Jpay system before we even left the parking lot.

"Ahmani, if I leave, you gotta make me a promise."

"What is it?" I asked.

"You gotta do everything you can to take care of Ira, I mean *whatever* he needs."

"You don't have to ask twice, I got him," I promised.

She stared at me long and hard until she was convinced of the truth in my words. Once she was satisfied, I started the car and drove away from the jail.

"As bad as I want to know where you're going, you can't tell me. I just want you to check in with me at least once a week so that I know you're alright," I said.

"I have no fucking *idea* where I'm going or how I'm gonna get there. I gotta pick up my house and…"

"No, you don't, I'm giving you enough money to buy whatever you need. All you gotta do is pack the shit that has sentimental value to you and Isaiah, and fuck everything else. As for transportation, we're getting ready to fix that problem now," I stated.

"Fix it how? I know damn well you're not about to give me your new Porsche."

"I could see me now trying to explain *that* to Katrina. Nah, I got something else in mind," I replied cryptically.

"Okay, so it sounds like you want me to leave today."

"The sooner the better is the idea, Amee, but don't worry I'll stay with you until you're sure that you have everything you need."

"What if I need something that can't be bought?" she asked softly.

I opened my mouth to tell her that I still had three hundred thousand dollars in the trunk of my car right now, but then I realized what she meant.

"Amee, I heard what you said when we got to the jail, and I understand why you said it. I'm not gonna keep playing with your emotions."

"I don't think you're playing with my emotions. I think we're drawn to each other in a way that probably wouldn't have been possible if things hadn't happened the way that they did. There's nothing wrong with beauty coming from tragedy," she replied.

"Yeah, but..."

"No buts, Ahmani. If I'm leaving for God knows where for God knows how long, then you and I are gonna share one last moment. End of discussion."

I didn't try to hide the smile on my face or the bulge in my jeans.

Chapter 9
One month later

"Ahmani, come on before you make me late!" Katrina hollered.

Any other time she didn't have a problem being late to get somewhere, especially if she wanted some dick, but since I was enjoying my leisure time she was in a hurry. I quickly fired the desert eagle .40 until the magazine was empty, and then I quickly put a new mag in. With the gun tucked into my slacks, I made my way back upstairs where I found a very pregnant lady stuffing her face with jelly donuts.

"How you gonna rush me and you're still eating?" I asked.

"Because I'm *always* eating, and we need to go because I can't be late for court. You're driving," she stated, making sure to grab two donuts on her food intake, violent mood swings, and sudden weight gain.

Of course, I wasn't allowed to comment on *any* of those things if I wanted my head to stay firmly on my shoulders, but the shit was comical at times. The morning that she woke up and couldn't see her feet reduced us both to tears for different reasons. I'd tried not to laugh in her face, but she'd been so dramatic with her facial expressions and tone that I couldn't help it, and when she'd started crying, I was really weak. Needless to say, I'd spent all day eating her pussy to make up for it.

"Why are you getting in the truck?" I asked.

"Because I'm not about to lose my breakfast in that Porsche," she replied, getting in the passenger seat of the new all black H3 Hummer she ordered.

That's how you knew when you had too much money, when you could simply order a car instead going to the lot and picking it out. The new hummer came fully loaded and sitting on thirty-two-inch rims, and it rode like I was driving a cloud. I climbed behind the wheel, and after putting my pistol in the center console, I navigated us out of the garage and toward the courthouse.

"Did you talk to Mr. Sprano?" I asked.

"Yeah, he's already at the courthouse because he had another case to handle before mine."

"I know his ass better be focused on your case, especially with the amount of money we've already kicked out," I said seriously.

"Oh, he's earning his money bae, especially because he's already said that I won't go to trial before our babies are born, and probably not for a while after."

"Are you sure that you wanna go to trial?" I asked.

"Ahmani, we've talked about this. I'm not taking a plea because I didn't do anything except defend us and our unborn children, and no jury in the world will convict me of a crime once they hear the circumstances."

"All I know is I've learned enough about myself to know that I wouldn't bet my future on the odds of a reasonable jury," I said truthfully.

"Not to sound uppity, bae, but you and I are different. This in one of those situations where I know how to use my white right."

I chuckled at this because I knew she was absolutely telling the truth. The jury really would be one of her peers, or at the very least those who would've done what she did in the same situation. The fact that the carjacker was just another nigga with a lengthy criminal record could only hurt her circumstances.

"What's the deal with Ira?" she asked suddenly.

"What do you mean?"

"I mean have they still not given him a bond or let him out?" she asked.

"No, and his P.O violated him. Plus, they still keep coming at him about that bullshit."

True to my word, I'd went on a fishing expedition with Katrina after Black Boy had told me of his suspicions with regards to her speaking his name, but nothing slipped out. I could only assume that he was paranoid.

"Ira is a killer, right?"

"I mean yeah, but…"

"And this dude was found tortured and shot in the neighborhood that Ira controls, right?" she persisted.

"Yeah, but…"

"So, then how is it not a logical deduction that he killed the man, Ahmani? I know Ira is your friend, but you yourself just spoke the truth about who he is," she said, taking my hand in hers.

I could tell that there was really no point in arguing with her, but it was on the tip of my tongue to point out that she didn't have a problem with who Black Boy was or what he did when it benefited her.

Deep down, I knew that she still felt some type of way about him refusing her last offer, but I thought she would've let it go once Aaron Charles had been forced to take a plea deal. Dude would spend the rest of his life in prison, and all the money in the world wouldn't keep him from grabbing his ankles before it was over.

"Agreeing to disagree is what makes marriages successful," I said.

"No, understanding that a happy wife equals a happy life is what makes a marriage successful."

I looked over at her to find her smiling right before stuffing her face with a donut. I had to laugh. Despite her fears we made it to the courthouse well before her scheduled 10 a.m. appearance, and in demonstration of my chivalrous side I'd offered to drop her off out front before I went and parked.

"I need you to do me a quick favor, baby," she said, smiling at me in a way that indicated refusal wasn't an option.

"Your wish is my command."

"Oooh, are you ready to bring role-playing into our bedroom activities? Ahmani, I saw some costumes online and…"

"Will you stay focused, you freak!" I said, laughing.

"Okay, but we're finishing this conversation later. Right now, I need you to run to McDonald's for me, and because you love me, I know you're not gonna judge me for it."

"I would never," I replied, sarcastically.

"You better not or you'll be on throat, pussy, and ass restriction," she threatened, smiling

We both knew that these words were hollow because she physically *needed* sex to keep her sanity during this pregnancy, but I didn't see the benefit to pointing this out right now.

"What do you want from McDonald's, sweetheart?"

"I want two sausage egg McGriddles, and four hash browns please," she replied happily.

"I got you," I said, leaning over and giving her a kiss.

I'd never understood how much work it took with regards to doing the little things to keep your woman happy, but I was learning more each day.

Once she'd climbed down out of the truck, I pulled off in search of the nearest McDonald's. The image of Katrina standing in front of the judge with one hand on her stomach while holding a hash brown in the other, entering a plea of not guilty, made me laugh out loud.

After ten minutes of driving, I found what I was looking for, and just as I pulled up to the drive-through my phone rang.

Recognizing the number from the jail phone had me answering quickly and pushing one without hesitation.

"What's up, bruh?" I asked.

"Same shit what up with you," Black Boy replied.

"Getting ready to go to court with my wife, but I'm making a run for one of her cravings right now."

"You talked to my lawyer recently?" he asked.

"Not in a couple weeks. Why?"

"He thinks them people might be trying to put something together on that one thing and come head hunting for me," he replied.

The lack of emotion or worry in his voice didn't fool me into believing he wasn't feeling the pressure because it was already understood what a murder charge would carry.

"What do you need me to do?" I asked.

"Go sit down with my lawyer and find out how serious this shit is. He'll talk to you because you're kickin' him that money."

"I'm on top of it with both feet, my nigga," I replied seriously.

"Look, I got somebody that wanna holla at you. You may not remember, but you know dude and you fuck with him. I mean you got to if you put five thousand dollars on his books," Black Boy said.

"Put him on."

"What's up, young nigga?" a voice asked, a few seconds later.

"Maintaining. Who is this?" I asked.

"Doug. But you always called me Old Man or Pops. I was kinda like your unofficial official tour guide the last time you were in here on those bogus charges."

"Oh, okay. Well, I appreciate what you did," I said sincerely.

"I knew that, you already went out of your way to show me your appreciation. I just can't believe all the shit that's happened to you since you left, it's like you passed off every black car in the world with the way you run into bad luck."

"I think I'm doing a'ight. I'm married to a bad bitch with plenty of money, I got a beautiful son and two more baby girls on the way. If that's bad luck, then I don't need to know what good luck looks like," I replied.

"Yeah, your brother told me that you'd lost your memory. Congratulations on the kids, though, I believe you'll be a good father. Can I give you a piece of free advice, though?"

"As long as you're not trying to put me on to a heist or nothing," I said, laughing.

"Nah, I wouldn't do no shit like that over the phone. I just want to tell you to keep your eyes open out there, and don't see what you wanna see, see what's really there. One more thing. I never really told you how much I appreciated our relationship, but I did and I still do. I love you, young nigga. Always."

I didn't know what to say to that, but before I could utter a word I heard him passing the phone back off.

"Only you can make lifelong friends while you're in jail fighting for your life," Black Boy said.

"Apparently. Keep an eye on dude for me, a'ight?"

"I'll handle shit in here, you just focus on shit out there. You heard from Amee?" he asked.

I wanted to tell him how bad it was killing me to only get a text from her here and there, but that was my new truth to wrestle with. I'd known I would miss her when she left, especially after the tender way we'd made love that last day, but I hadn't expected it to be this bad.

"She texts once a week like I told her to, but I haven't actually talked to her since she left," I replied.

"Damn, my nigga it sounds like you in pain. Guess that pussy is as good as I thought."

"Man, fuck you," I said, determined not to feed into his laughter.

"Real shit, though, is she good?"

"Yeah. I bought her a brand new 2017 Ford Explorer, gave her one hundred thousand dollars, and put her and Isaiah on the road," I replied.

"Did you hit one more time and tell her you loved her?"

"Man, *fuck you!*" I repeated, laughing this time.

"It's okay, my nigga, you've *always* had a thing for Amee, you just never had the balls to take it there. I guess getting shot in the head will make you fearless, though, huh?"

"Or foolish because now I'm over here punch drunk about a woman that *ain't* my wife," I said, shaking my head.

"Trust me, bruh, Amee is better for you, all the money in the world can't buy what she'll give you."

I could tell by his tone that he felt like he was speaking the truth, but his words only added to the confusion my emotions were swimming in.

"I need to get this pregnant lady her food before she blows the courthouse down, but I'll go see your lawyer a.s.a.p.," I said.

"A'ight. I'll call you in a few days."

We disconnected our call, and I drove through the drive-through and got Katrina's food. My mind stayed on Amee, though. Despite what Black Boy had said, I knew it wasn't all about the sex between her and I, and he'd kind of eluded to it when he said I'd always had a thing for her. I didn't know if that was true, but I knew the friendship that she'd described between us was the type of foundation that you could build forever on. That didn't mean that I was questioning my connection with Katrina or why we'd moved so fast. I just knew that I was trying to find myself, and there didn't seem to be a woman in the world who knew me better than Amee did. I tried to block all that from my mind as I parked, grabbed Katrina's food, and hopped out. I'd almost made the mistake of grabbing my gun, but trying to bring that in the courthouse guaranteed that my next meal would be shared with Black Boy.

"Bae, what *took* you so long?" Katrina asked, obviously frustrated.

"You're really gonna get mad at me because McDonald's had a line? Like you wouldn't have been twice as pissed if I would've gone to Burger King instead."

A sheepish look quickly spread over her face, and the moment she bit into a hash brown all was forgiven.

"I'm sorry, my wonderful amazing husband, you were right, and I appreciate you doing what I asked. I'll make it up to you later," she promised.

"Yes, you will. Now where's your lawyer?"

"Talking to the district attorney, but he said that I might not even have to appear in court today," she replied.

"So, what the fuck did we rush all the way down here for?" I asked angrily.

"Ahmani, why are you yelling at me like I knew all of this ahead of time? You act like I *wanna* be going through this shit at all, but remember whose idea it was to be in Georgetown South in the first damn place."

"Forgive me for insisting that you know the man you're married to. I won't make that mistake again," I said sarcastically.

The flame in her eyes told me that this fight was about to take on several shades of ugliness, which would only make me look like a piece of shit for fighting with a pregnant woman in public. Thankfully, my ringing phone provided a timely distraction, allowing me an excuse to step away from her while pulling it out to answer the call.

"Yo?" I said, without looking to see who the savior on the other end was.

"Hey."

The sound of her voice immediately gave me tunnel vision, and all I could see in that bright light was her.

"Amee?" I whispered.

"Yeah, it's me."

"What's wrong?" I asked, moving further out of Katrina's range of hearing, even though I knew she'd question me later.

"Nothing's wrong, I just wanted to hear your voice.

"You sure that's all it is, sweetheart? You sound weird," I said.

"I guess I'm homesick. I mean, I've lived in Virginia my whole life, and I was always around someone I knew, but now I'm out here in the world all alone. It doesn't feel good Ahmani, it feels like I've been banished for no reason."

I could hear a range of emotions in her voice, and her loneliness was palpable, which made my heart ache.

"Amee, you're never alone because I'm with you wherever you go, and so is Black Boy. Matter fact, he just asked about you when I talked to him a little while ago,"

"How is he?" she asked.

"Maintaining. I'm going to see his lawyer today so that I can get an update."

"Tell him that I love him the next time you talk to him," she said.

"I will."

For long seconds, a silence hung between us, but I didn't know if I was supposed to be the one to break it. There was so much I wanted to say, but I knew that I couldn't because I shouldn't.

"If I asked you to do something for me, would you do it?" she asked.

"Yes."

"You said that too quick Ahmani, and you better think about it because you don't know what I'm gonna ask," she said, laughing.

"It doesn't matter, the answer is still yes."

"Will you come see me?" she asked softly.

"Where are you?"

"I'm in Puerto Rico, but..."

"I'll be there a.s.a.p."

Chapter 10

"You'll be *where* a.s.a.p.?" Katrina asked, from right behind me.

"Oh, shit," Amee said in my ear.

"Hold on for a second, please," I said, calmly, into the phone before turning around to give Katrina my full attention.

"I'm on the phone with Black Boy's lawyer, just give me a minute," I replied.

I could tell by the look in her eyes that it didn't matter who I was on the phone with, she was gonna stand right here next to me.

"Okay, I'm back," I said into my phone, while discreetly turning the volume down.

Is she still standing there?" Amee asked.

"Absolutely," I replied.

"Ahmani, I'm sorry, I shouldn't have called and I shouldn't have asked…"

"But you *did* do both of those things, and that's what's important as far as I'm concerned. I know that you wouldn't have called and asked to see me if it wasn't serious, so when is a good time for you?" I asked, watching Katrina as closely as she was watching me.

"As soon as possible sounds great to me," Amee replied.

I could already hear the difference in her voice compared to a little while ago, and that made me want to smile, but I knew that I had to suppress it.

"Then were in agreement. I'll call you after I find out what's going on with my wife's court appearance," I said.

"Be safe, Ahmani. I love you."

"The same to you," I replied, hanging up and blowing out an exhaustive breath as if I was tired of being bothered.

"What was that all about?" Katrina asked, taking a bite of her breakfast sandwich.

"Just a bunch of tedious bullshit. Black Boy needs character witnesses at his hearing for his violation, along with proof that he has a steady job."

"Okay. This concerns you how?" she asked.

"Because, obviously, I agreed to be a character witness, plus I said that he was employed at the tattoo shop. Amee was supposed to be his other witness, but the lawyer said that he hadn't been able to get in contact with her."

"Have you spoken to her?" she asked casually, with just enough concern to make me believe that she really cared.

"Nah, I ain't talked to or seen her since the cookout, and I don't got time to go looking for her," I replied, putting my phone back in my pocket.

"You're right about that because the only woman that you need to be chasing behind is my pregnant ass. Listen, bae, we gotta have open communication in this relationship because I don't like stumbling up on information that should come directly from you unsolicited. Whatever your involvement is with helping Ira, I think I should know about it, especially when it involving our business," she stated reasonably.

"I apologize, babe," I replied, pulling her into my arms and kissing her forehead softly.

The lack of tension in her body allowed me to breathe a sigh of relief, but my mind was quickly back to work trying to figure out how the fuck I was gonna up and go to Puerto Rico. No excuse was immediately coming to mind, but I was absolutely determined to figure something out.

"Your lawyer still ain't come out and told you nothing new?" I asked.

"No, not yet."

"You know what we need, we need a vacation," I said, smiling enticingly at her.

"Mmm, that sounds *wonderful.* Lay on the beach all day, and make love on that same sand at night," she replied wishfully.

"So, let's do it, then, baby, let's get away for a while."

"Bae, you don't gotta twist my arm for me to be on board, but maybe you can enlighten me as to how we're gonna travel to a beautiful, exotic location when I had to give up my passport," she said.

I knew the look of disappointment riding my face matched hers, but mine was just a play while I did a slow thirty second count in my head.

"We could always do the next best thing and go to Puerto Rico, I head its beautiful there," I said casually.

"You've never been? Baby, it's *gorgeous* there, and you're right we could go because it's technically part of the United States."

"I'll take care of the arrangements, while you take care of your business," I said, nodding toward the lawyer headed in our direction.

"Alright, so the good news is that your preliminary hearing had been put on hold while they look into that information we discussed, so there's no court today. I do need your signature on some paperwork though," Mr. Sprano said.

"What information are they looking into?" I asked.

"It's just some more background on the dude I shot, babe, nothing important. Do you have the papers you need me to sign?" she asked, stepping out of my arms.

"We can take care of it right in this room," he replied, indicating a door a few feet away.

"Ahmani, I'll be right back."

Part of me wanted to go with her to make sure that everything was straight, but I knew I had to act fast since I'd got her to agree to go to Puerto Rico. I quickly pulled my phone out and called Amee back.

"Hello?"

"It's me. I've got good news and bad news," I said rapidly.

"Okay."

"I'm coming to Puerto Rico, but Katrina is coming with me. I couldn't think of a logical reason to disappear for days, and I didn't need her getting suspicious," I said, keeping eyes on the door that my wife had gone through, in anticipation of her return.

For a moment, the line between me and Amee hummed silently, and I was afraid that she hung up the phone.

"When will you be here?" she asked finally.

"By tomorrow, at the latest. I've gotta check in with Black Boys lawyer, but I'm gonna book the flight as soon as possible."

"Okay well, call me when you get here," she replied.

"I will, sweetheart, I'm looking forward to seeing you," I said honestly.

"Me too, we've got a lot of catching up to do."

"Oh *really?*" I asked.

"Get your mind out of the gutter, nigga, you're bringing pussy with you so you don't need mine."

"Bullshit!" I blurted out loudly, causing people to look at me like I was crazy.

I didn't care, though, because it was just good to hear Amee laugh again.

"We're not about to have this argument now, I'll see you when you get here," she replied, still chuckling.

"Uh huh, stop acting like you ain't bout to give me some because we both know what it is."

"Bye, boy," she said, hanging up.

I was still smiling as I dialed the number to get Black Boy's lawyer on the phone. Tobias Fraisure was a beast when it came to criminal defense, which was why he cost so damn much. Being that I was his most current money machine his receptionist put me through without hesitation.

"Mr. Monroe, how can I help you today?" he asked.

"I just spoke to Ira not too long ago, and he's concerned about his name being, linked to that Robert Cook homicide."

"Yeah, I'm looking into that myself because I don't like all the whispers and the side eye, but if they have something on it, they're guarding it close," he replied.

"Put an investigator on it if you have to, Tobias, I'll pay for it because it's worth it not to get blindsided."

"I'll take care of it, and grease the necessary wheels. I'll also go to the jail today and visit Ira, personally," he said.

"That sounds like a plan. I'm getting ready to go out of town for a few days, but I'll have my phone on me so hit me up if you find out something," I replied.

"Will do."

I hung up the phone and immediately started checking for flights times to get us on our way to a much-needed vacation. By the time Katrina returned, I had everything situated, and I was just anxious to get gone.

"You ready?" I asked.

"Yep, we're good to go. Did you check on the necessary arrangements for our trip?"

"Check on it? Bae, the flight and villa are booked, and the car is rented. We've got three hours to pack and get to Dulles international airport," I replied smiling.

"Whoa, you're moving just a *little* too fast because you're obviously forgetting some things."

Such as?" I asked.

"Baby, I'm out on *bond*, I can't just vanish into thin air. I just told the lawyer to get it approved for me to be able to go, but that could take a few days. Plus, he needs to make sure that there isn't anything else that I need to sign."

"What are you signing? Is he explaining everything to you because I don't want you putting your name on something that's gonna come back to bite you in the ass later," I said seriously.

"Ahmani, I'm not stupid, okay? I know what I'm doing."

I hadn't meant to insult her intelligence, but the attitude now contorting her face said that I'd done just that. "I know you're not stupid baby, I'm just a concerned husband. As for the trip I'll reschedule everything," I said.

"Actually, I think that you should go ahead and I'll meet you there in a few days."

"Huh?" I asked, not believing my ears enough to trust what I'd just heard.

"I said that you should go down there first. Bae, you know how cranky and moody I've been, so it would really help me to relax if you went ahead and had everything waiting for me when I got there. I don't want to be stressed in the slightest on our vacation," she replied.

It was hard for me not to hop out of my skin while listening to here give me what I'd actually been scheming to get the whole time, but I kept a straight face.

"If that's what you want me to do, baby, I'll do it."

"And that's why I love you," she said, wrapping her arms around my neck and pulling my lips to hers.

"Is there anything that you need me to do before I leave?"

"Well, the first thing that you need to do is call you P.O to make sure that he doesn't have a problem with you leaving, and then you need to take me home and fuck me like you're gonna miss me," she replied, smiling.

"Yes, ma'am."

I kissed her quickly before taking her hand and leading her outside to the truck. I made the call to my probation officer as I drove home and got the necessary permission to leave the state, while Katrina changed my flight information.

"Of course, you would rent a damn Ferrari, wouldn't you?" She asked, shaking her head.

"Bae, it was *you* who introduced me to fast cars."

"Don't remind me. You're still booked on the same flight, and mine is booked for three days from now. I figure that should be enough time," she said.

"So, what kind of food do you want me to have waiting for you?"

"Sweets, of course, but if you're gonna cook for me then you already know what I like," she replied.

"Yeah, meat," I said laughing.

"Smartass!" Even as she said this, though, her hand was reaching for the zipper to my pants, and before I knew it, I was receiving a masterful hand job.

"Bae, I'm trying to drive."

"I'm not stopping you from driving, I mean it's not like I'm sucking your dick," she replied, moving her hand faster.

"Smartass."

Now, it was her turn to laugh. I managed to get us home in one piece, and then I spent the next two hours making her pay for the torture she'd put me through. I fucked her so good that when it came time for me to get ready to leave, she couldn't get out of the bed to drive me to the airport.

After spending time with my son and promising Katrina that I would call as soon as I landed, I hopped in my car and made the drive to the airport, arriving with only fifteen minutes to spare. Luckily, I only had a carry-on bag so I was able to make it through security and board my flight quickly.

Once I was buckled in with a glass of Henny to get rid of my nerves about flying, I sent Amee a text to let her know that I was on my way. Alone. Even through the message, I could feel her immediate relief. I agreed to call her once I get to my villa, then I kicked my feet up and relaxed.

Within minutes, the captain came over the intercom and gave his little speech, and then we were taking off. Having never been on a plane, I wasn't prepared for the takeoff.

One minute we were rolling along at a nice relaxing speed and then the speed changed to *oh hell nah* in the blink of an eye! Even after the plane made its climb and leveled off, I wasn't feeling this mode of transportation, but miraculously I was able to fall asleep. I don't know how long I stayed that way before a rather large bump jolted me awake, but I looked out the window to find myself back on the ground alive. That was definitely a cause for celebration.

Thirty minutes later, I was behind the wheel of my rented Ferrari headed for a villa near the beach. Despite the expensive cost of the rental, seeing the breath-taking view of the ocean through the floor to ceiling windows made it all worth it. I'd never seen water so blue. Even at night, it was mesmerizing to watch the waves move to and fro. I was definitely a long way from the hood. After texting Amee my address I took a quick shower, and ordered some food. When a knock came at the door, I thought that it was the food because it'd only ten minutes, but I opened the door to a much more beautiful sight.

"Hey, stranger," I said, opening my arms to her.

"Hey yourself."

It felt good to hold her and imprint her sweet scent on my memory to take back home with me.

"Where's Isaiah?" I asked, leading her inside and closing the door.

"He's staying with his new friend for the night."

"It's good that he's making friends out here," I said.

"I'm not so sure because this friend is a girl," she replied, wrinkling up her face in displeasure.

I had to laugh, even though it earned me some side eye.

"Relax, Amee, he's still shooting blanks."

"Yeah, but you're obviously not," she said.

"I *know*! Twins! My mom didn't warn me that they ran in the family," I replied, leading her to the balcony where we could enjoy the view.

"Twins?"

"Yeah, I told you that Katrina is having twin girls, right?" I asked.

"No, you forgot that."

"Oh, I thought that's what you meant when you said…"

"No, I wasn't talking about your wife, Ahmani. I'm talking about the baby I'm carrying."

Aryanna

Chapter 11

"I'm sorry, can you repeat that because it *sounded* like you said you're pregnant," I replied, taking a seat.

"Yeah, that's what I said."

"Amee you can't be pregnant."

"Tell that to my uterus," she said sarcastically.

"No, I mean you *can't* be pregnant. You always said that you couldn't have any more kids."

"I know because that's what the doctors told me after I had Isaiah, and since its never happened in the last ten years, I never said anything to you since you got shot about me not being able to have a baby. The only conversation we had about that was years ago! You-you remember?" she asked.

I could hear the hope in her voice and see it in every beautiful line on her face, but I still wondered how she would accept the truth I'd come to tell her.

"Yes, I remember."

"Oh, my God, that's amazing!" She said, excitedly, flinging herself into my arms.

"Amee, wait, we need to talk."

"Ahmani, the baby…"

"No, that's not what we need to talk about," I said hesitantly.

"Okay. What is it?" she asked, pulling back so that she could look at me, but not moving from the seat she'd taken on my leg.

I took a deep breath knowing that I had no clue how this situation was about to play out.

"I didn't just come out here because you asked me to come, or because I missed you. The truth is that I've been yearning to talk to you ever since you and Isaiah left."

"Have you had your memory back that long?" she asked.

"Longer. Amee, I never lost my memory."

At first, she just stared at me like she hadn't heard a word I'd said, blinking real slowly and licking her lips.

"Say that again," she said.

"I never lost my memory. I only said that because…"

I never got the reason out of my mouth before she hit me with a stunning right hook to the jaw. I thought that she might've been coming with a follow up, but she simply got up and stormed off.

"Amee, wait I…"

"Fuck you, Ahmani!" she yelled, walking out the door without another look.

I always knew this could be one of the ways she would react, no matter how good my reasons were for my deception. There had never been any lies between us in our relationship, and now I'd told one hell of one that had literally *changed* everything between us. Amee had been one of my best friends for my entire life, and now when we should be celebrating the joys of new life, we were virtually strangers.

A sudden knock at the door had me on my feet and moving, hoping she'd come back to hear me out, but it was just the food I'd ordered.

After signing for it, I left it untouched on the table and tried to figure out how to fix this mess I'd made. The only option that I had left was the truth. Pulling my phone out, I sat down to compose a text to Amee, hoping that she would read it and not simply throw her phone in the ocean.

For fifteen minutes, I let my fingers dance across my phones screen, baring my soul in a way that I hadn't with anyone, not even Elyse. I understood that no justification would take away the sting of a lie, but I needed Amee to understand that what I'd done hadn't come from malicious intent. I needed her to understand that my love for her was real. Once it was sent, I knew that there was nothing more that I could do, so I put my phone drown and went in search of something to make me forget. I had a sneaky suspicion that the bottle of Bacardi 151 I found at the bar would be just what the doctor ordered. I was on my third glass by the time my ringing phone got my attention.

"Hello?" I slurred.

"Ahmani, is that you?"

"Yes, Katrina, its me."

"Why do you sound like that? What's wrong?" she asked concerned.

It was on the tip of my tongue to ask her if she meant *besides* the fact that she had my family killed, but I wasn't that drunk. Yet.

"It was my first time flying, and I needed a little liquid courage."

"Sounds like you had more than a little, bae. Where are you?" she asked.

"At the villa, where else would I be?"

"Okay smartass, well sleep it off and call me in the morning. I love you," she replied.

"Love you, too."

When I hung up, I took another drink because I always hated the taste those words left in my mouth. The only way I'd been able to endure saying and demonstrating love for her was by acknowledging the truth that all my actions were motivated by hate.

My hatred for Katrina was immeasurable, and it pumped through my body like the blood that kept me alive. Hate and revenge were the driving forces behind everything I did when it came to Katrina. Amee had been the balance to that, though, the anchor to make sure that I didn't get consumed by the fire I was playing with and implode before my plan reached its fruition. Amee was my sunshine in this perfect storm that I was caught in. Thinking about her had me looking at the phone in my hand, fighting against the desperate need that I felt to call her. Another knock at the door interrupted those thoughts though, and had me moving slowly to answer.

"No more food," I said, pulling the door open.

At first, I thought that I must be a lot more drunk than I originally suspected, but Amee's hand on my chest made me know that she wasn't a figment of my imagination. She gently pushed me backwards until she could shut the door behind her. For what seemed like an eternity we simply stood there staring at each other, speaking without speaking. In this moment there was no alcohol clouding my mind, but her nearness was making me intoxicated in a different way.

"Amee I…"

"Make love to me," she said, taking my hand and leading me back out to the balcony.

The night air was cool and the sounds of the ocean were hypnotic. The moonlights reflection in Amee's green eyes had me in a trance as she allowed me to slowly lift the thin cotton of the dress she was wearing up and over her head. Despite us being secluded from prying eyes I felt like her body was too beautiful to share with even the creatures of the night. I wanted to ravish her, but I remained patient by allowing her to undress me.

Once there were no clothes between us, I took her face gently in my hands and reintroduced out lips to one another. The spark of electricity was instant and only became more pronounced as the seconds ticked by.

"Hold onto me," I whispered against her lips.

Grabbing two handfuls of her firm ass cheeks, I lifted her up onto the concrete wall that enclosed the balcony, and stepped in between her thick thighs. My dick was already pounding like the music that I could hear in the distance, but still I took my time when it came to making the two of us one whole. My rhythm was slow and steady as I held her body close to mine, taking us on a journey of past and future.

"I love you," I whispered into her ear.

"I love you, too," she sighed, locking her legs around me.

I could feel her nails digging into the flesh of my back as my strokes became more forceful, but that didn't deter me from my mission. When my lips locked onto her neck and I started sucking, her moans took on a girlish quality, but I know that the dick I was giving her had her feeling real grown. Harder and harder her pussy throbbed under my direct assault until suddenly it could take no more, and the sounds of her climax were accompanying music to the waves crashing in the distance. Knowing that she was still feeling aftershocks, I quickly put her back on her feet before spinning her around.

"I want to remember this moment forever," I said, bending her over slightly and pushing back inside of her.

I didn't move fast or try to pound her into submission, but instead my explorations intensity matched the beauty surrounding us.

"Oh God! Ahmani!" She cried out passionately.

I let my hands move up and down her body, seeking to stimulate her completely while pushing her to heights unknown. Her body spoke to me like old friends and even older lovers, allowing me to push her over the cliff of her second orgasm in ten minutes. The way her legs trembled made her ass jiggle in a way that tested my control, but I remained focused.

"Come here," I said, pulling out of her, and leading her to a lounge chair.

I laid down and she trailed me, quickly sliding my dick back inside the safety of her heart and tightness.

"Make me cum," I challenged.

When she leaned forward to kiss me I thought that she was gonna use the same gentleness that I had when making her cum, but I was wrong. Suddenly, she was popping her pussy on my dick with speed and determination. When I opened my mouth to tell her to slow down, she swiveled her hips again and again, making talking impossible.

For ten solid minutes, she alternated between riding me hard and fast, to painfully slow. By the time we finally came together, I was sure some people heard us back in Virginia. It was still another five minutes before my breathing was under control enough to talk.

"So, does this mean that you forgive me?" I asked.

"I don't know yet. Ask me later."

"I really am sorry for lying to you," I said, sincerely.

She didn't reply right away, but she didn't move from where she was laying on my chest, and my dick was still inside her. These were positive things. I wrapped my arms around her and enjoyed feeling the beat of her heart against my chest.

"Part of me knew," she said softly.

"How?"

"Because you never looked at me like a stranger, not even that first day I saw you at the cemetery. Your look was blank, like you were masking your thoughts," she replied.

"I was, especially when Katrina froze up at the sight of you two. I didn't expect you all to be there, but I knew immediately what Black Boy's reaction would be."

"You took a serious risk pulling a gun on him," she said.

"That's what tipped him off and had him waiting for me outside your house the next morning."

"Wait, so Ira knows that you're full of shit?" she asked, raising her head to look me in the eye.

"Yeah. The morning I left your house we talked and I let him know that I had a plan, but everybody had to be cool until Katrina had the baby. He agreed, and I filled him in as time went on."

The way that she was staring at me made me think that I was about to get punched again, but she eventually laid her head back on my chest and allowed me to go back to holding her.

"The first time that we had sex you looked at me with so much love that I thought that there was no way you didn't remember me, but I couldn't see why you'd lie about that," she said.

"I know how truly crazy Katrina is. When I woke up in the hospital and saw her sleeping by my bedside, I knew immediately that whatever trickery she was on was still working if she wasn't in handcuffs. From what I'd been told, the text messages that her ex had were enough to cause reasonable doubt *and* cast suspicion in her direction. Then the fact that Elyse was dead after being cut wide open, I mean that should've had her in handcuffs too, but she wasn't. So, I decided to play dumb and see what I could figure out. It became really clear that playing dumb was my best offense and defense, because it allowed me to plot right under her nose," I admitted.

"God, you were *good,* though, especially when it came to me. The Ahmani that I know would *never* pursue me sexually, so when you did it threw me off, and the fact that it was good sex further distracted me."

"So, it's just *good*?" I asked smiling.

"Boy, now is *not* the time for you to be fishing for compliments on your dick. You're still in the dog house with me for lying!"

"A'ight, well let me tell you the truth, then. I love you Amee, and I've always loved you. Part of me was blind to how great we'd be together, and the other part of me was scared to find out. One thing I realized when I saw you at the cemetery is that life was too short for me not to find out what could happen between us. I did *not* foresee you getting pregnant though," I said seriously.

"Imagine my fucking shock when I finally realized my food poisoning was actual morning sickness!"

"When did you find out?" I asked, rubbing her back gently.

"A few days ago. I'm only like five weeks, so it's still early."

"You're not thinking of getting rid of it, are you?" I asked nervously.

"I can see that you want me to punch you in your muthafuckin' face again. Hell nah, I ain't getting rid of my baby! Even though your wife *did* kill your last baby mama," she replied seriously.

"I'm not gonna let Katrina do *anything* to you, or Isaiah. What happened to Elyse happened because I didn't know who Katrina really was, but I'm fully aware now. I'll protect you with my life."

"That's kind of hard for you to do when I'm way out here," she replied.

"That's why as soon as Katrina gets here you and Isaiah are leaving, but I don't want you to go back to Virginia I want you to go to Maryland. But you can't tell *nobody* where you are Amee, not even your family. We'll get you a house in a nice neighborhood, and you can lay low."

"Will you be coming to visit me?" she asked.

"Every chance I get."

"I'll do it under one condition. You gotta make sure that I've got guns to protect myself," she said, looking me in the eyes.

"Do you even know how to shoot a gun?" I asked.

"I'm a fast learner, and we both know that you're a good teacher of many things."

The smile on her face when she made that statement made me kiss her lovingly.

"Not so fast, negro, we still have shit to get straight," she said.

"I'm listening," I replied, putting my hands on her ass, and holding her steady while pushing up inside her slowly.

"Ahmani, I'm serious."

"Me too, I'm listening, baby," I mumbled, continuing to move.

"I'm having your baby, but are we gonna be together?"

"Yes, always," I whispered.

"Promise?" She moaned, now mixing with me.

"I promise, baby, anything you want." She suddenly stopped moving and stared at me intently.

"Don't ever make me a promise that you can't keep Ahmani."

"Amee, I love you, so if I make you a promise, I'm gonna keep it."

"Good, then you belong to me now," she said, resuming her movements.

"Uh huh."

"Say it, Ahmani, say it," she demanded, riding me faster.

"I belong to you."

"Say it like you mean it!" she growled, squeezing my dick mercilessly within her pussy walls.

"I belong to you, bae!"

Aryanna

Chapter 12

I'd officially been in Puerto Rico twenty-four hours, and I'd gotten *maybe* three hours of sleep. Amee knowing the truth about everything unlocked Pandora's box and emptied that bad mufucka when it came to how insatiable she was. We'd fucked so many ways in so many places all over the villa that I knew it would need a *thorough* cleaning before Katrina arrived.

Of course, I still had no idea when that would be though because when she called me to tell me Amee picked that *exact* moment to put my dick in her mouth. Even now I couldn't remember the excuse that I'd made to get off the phone, but I'd definitely insisted that Amee finish what she'd started. We'd probably be in a compromising position right now if she hadn't had to go make sure that her son was good, and not on his way to making her a grandmother. I used the down time to take a nice relaxing shower, and the plan now was to enjoy the view while I waited on my lunch to be brought to me. Having money made everything easier and more convenient, which was why I'd been able to keep fucking Amee while the help did the grocery shopping for me. I could've cooked myself lunch because the kitchen was stocked, but I was feeling lazy and content.

As if on cue I heard a knock at the door, signaling the arrival of my lobster salad. I made sure to grab a few dollars for a tip on my way to the door since I'd forgotten the courtesy the first night.

"Right on time," I said, taking the tray and passing the young Spanish dude the money.

"Gracias."

"De nada," I replied.

"Did you get enough for me?" Katrina asked, stepping out from where she'd been hiding, and pushing her way in the room.

"Uh, if you would've told me that you were coming, I would've ordered you something," I replied, fighting hard to remain calm.

"Yeah, well I tried to have a conversation with you about when I was coming out here, but you seemed *really* distracted," she said, looking around like she was expecting to find someone.

Suddenly she was headed toward the bedroom like a bloodhound with a fresh scent, leaving me to deal with her bag in the hallway. The waiter was nice enough to put it inside the door before retreating the way he'd come. I took my food onto the balcony so I could eat and enjoy the view while Inspector Gadget looked for clues. Thankfully, the maid had already been here to make the bed and change the towels, so my only real concern was the smell of good sex on a few surfaces around the villa. By the time Katrina made it to the balcony I was kicked back eating my food.

"You don't look happy to see me, Ahmani."

"That's because this is the first time, I'm actually *seeing* you, sweetheart. Your first priority was to toss the room, so did you find what you were looking for?"

"Don't be an asshole, did you miss me or not?" She asked impatiently.

I put my food down and stood slowly.

"Of course, I missed you," I replied, grabbing her by the throat and pulling her toward me roughly.

"Ahmani."

"Shhh. Answer my question, baby, did you find what you were looking for?" I whispered sweetly.

"No," she croaked.

"Ah."

I let her go and just stood there staring at her. To her this was a game of sexual domination, but in real life it was me letting a little of my anger out in a way that was degrading to her. Had she not been carrying my children I would've killed her a thousand different ways by now, and probably mutilated her body too.

For now, I'd settle for slutting her out. I pushed my shorts and boxers down, and put my hands on my hips expectantly while never wavering with my eye contact. It was obvious that she learned from our last encounter because she quickly got on her knees, sniffed my dick, and then took all of it in her mouth.

Normally, she insisted that I didn't grab her head, but she put both my hands on her head and looked up at me with blue eyes communicating the desire to please me. I allowed her to start off slow, but once my dick was harder than a burnt biscuit, I was ramming that mufucka to the back of her throat like I was throwing darts. She gagged a few times simply because of the force, but the tears in her eyes didn't mask her hunger. For a moment I was completely caught up with fucking Katrina's face, but all of a sudden, I got the feeling that we weren't alone.

Looking past Katrina back into the villa, I could just make out a figure in the shadows, and it was a figure I knew well. I could feel Katrina trying to turn her head, signaling my distraction, but I held onto her firmly and moaned like she was giving me the best head of my life. I watched in horror as Amee moving silently toward us, not knowing what the fuck I was supposed to do other than get my dick sucked. When Amee got close enough for me to read her facial expression I was surprised to find it completely blank, but I was more shocked by the fact that she was actually standing there watching. As precarious as this moment was, the fact that I was fighting not to cum forced me to acknowledge how erotic I was finding it. Amee stopped watching Katrina long enough to look me in the eyes.

"I love you, I promise, I said passionately.

For s split second, she just looked at me, but then she mouthed the words *I love you too* and blew me a kiss. As quietly as she entered, Amee retraced her step and left my keycard on the table before vanishing. Only then did I pull my dick from between Katrina's lips and shoot thick globs of cum all over her face.

"You got it in my nose," she complained, swiftly backing away.

I chuckled softly, pulled my pants up, and sat back down to finish my lunch while she cussed and went in search of the bathroom. I got my phone and quickly sent Amee a text explaining what she'd walked in on, and telling her that I wanted to see her before her and Isaiah got on the road. The sound of Katrina approaching forced me to send my message quickly and tuck my phone.

"Baby, I'm hungry," Katrina whined.

"Would you like me to cook for you or do you wanna go out?"

"As drunk as you were, I'm surprised you went shopping already," she commented.

"Trust me, baby, I've used my time in Puerto Rico wisely, even with a hangover," I replied, smiling, genuinely.

"Well, in that case I would love it if you cooked for me."

I sat my plate down, stood up and took her hand, and led her into the kitchen with me.

"Grab a seat and tell me what's going on with your case," I said, pulling out a stool for her to sit on, before going to the refrigerator.

"Well, Mr Sprano actually thinks I have a good chance of beating it."

"Really? I thought he wanted you to take a plea," I replied.

"Oh, he knows by now. That I'm not even about to consider that, so he's been working overtime to get me off."

"Are you saying that you're fucking your lawyer Katrina?"

"Ha ha smart ass, you know the answer to that question," she sneered.

I laughed at the expression on her face while pulling out everything I needed to make her a turkey sandwich.

"Baby, I thought you were *cooking* for me," she whined.

I truly wanted to pick her up and slam her head first into floor, but I kept my husbandly smile in place.

"Bae, I *am* gonna cook for you, but I'm making spaghetti. Since that's gonna take a little while I thought that I would make you a sandwich so you wouldn't be so hangry."

"Oh," she replied with a sheepish smile.

"I'm sorry, Ahmani, I should've known that you were being thoughtful. My mind is just a mess right now."

"That's why you've got me here to vent to, so finish telling me about these moves your lawyer is making," I said.

"Well, one thing that we discussed is moving my trial date up instead of pushing it back."

"How come?" I asked, passing her the sandwich I'd made her.

"Because the imagery of me being pregnant with twins will be too much for the judge and jury to ignore."

I had to give her props for what she'd told me the other day, she definitely knew how to use her white right.

"That could actually work. What else is he planning?" I asked.

"I don't know, you know that good lawyers are full of all kinds of legal tricks."

I felt my phone vibrating in my pocket, but I was smart enough not to pull it out in front of Katrina because it was probably Amee.

"I want you to hurry up and eat that sandwich bae because I'm putting you to work when I come back from the bathroom," I said, giving her a quick kiss on the nose.

"Is that supposed to make up for you shooting cum straight to my brain?"

I laughed even as I kept walking. Once I was secluded behind the bathroom door, I pulled my phone out and read Amee's text message. I didn't need to look in the mirror to know that I was frowning, and I wasted no time calling her ass either.

"What do you mean that you don't think it's a good idea?" I whispered, once she answered.

"Ahmani, you know that it's not a good idea for you to sneak out to see me. If I hadn't left to check on Isaiah your wife would've caught us instead of me catching you two."

"Amee, *you're* my wife in every way that counts," I whispered fiercely.

"If that's truly how you feel then you need to be thinking about what's best for me, Isaiah, and the baby I'm carrying now, *not* what will make Ahmani feel better. You know how dangerous that bitch is, so act like it."

It was so hard for me not to point out how quick she'd been to ignore that danger when she stood not ten feet away from the *same* bitch in question, and watched her eat my dick like it was Thanksgiving! The only thing that kept me from saying what I was thinking was the fact that she was right, even if she was being hypocritical.

"When are you leaving?" I asked, still whispering.

"By tomorrow we'll be on the move, so keep her out here as long as you can. I'm sure that you two can stay busy."

"Amee, I'm sorry…"

"I love you, Ahmani," she said, hanging up the phone.

I wanted to call her back and keep calling until she answered, but I knew that all I would succeed in doing is starting a fight I couldn't win, and make Katrina suspicious, too. As hard as it was, I put my phone in my pocket, took a piss, washed my hands, and went back to the kitchen.

"Perfect timing, what do you want me to do?" Katrina asked, wiping the crumbs from her mouth.

The word *die* was on the tip of my tongue, but of course I didn't say it.

"I want you to cut up the green pepper and mushroom while I cut up the onion, that way I can fry everything in the pan with the sausage."

"I can do that," she replied, moving to the kitchen table.

"So, babe, I've been thinking about what I wanna do with my life. I know that you don't mind me being a kept man, but I wanna be more than that."

"What we're thinking about doing?" she asked curiously.

"I've actually been taking some online business courses."

"Really?" she asked, unable to hide the complete shock on her face.

"Really. I mean I ain't no dummy and I made good grades in school, so I figured I could learn something new if I applied myself."

"I don't know what to say. I mean that's *great,* baby, why didn't you tell me sooner?" she asked, getting excited.

"Because I wanted to be sure that it was something I wanted to stick with. I didn't wanna get your hopes up, and then I tried it, but didn't like it."

"So, is this why you bought the tattoo shop?" she asked.

"In part. The idea of buying property and flipping it appeals to me more than running something on a daily basis. Buying and flipping is just like selling dope, but on a larger scale."

She laughed out loud at that and nodded her head in agreement.

"You know, my dad was in real estate, which is kinda in the same vein as what you're describing," she said.

"You probably told me that, but I don't remember, bae. Is it hard to do?"

"I mean there are classes for that just like anything else in the world, but baby you're a natural born hustler so I know you'll pick that shit up in your sleep," she replied encouragingly.

"I'm glad you have faith in me. What I'll do is look into what types of classes I can take and absorb all the information that I can, then I'll get the financial backing I need to-."

"What are you talking about financial backing? Bae, we're *rich*, remember?" She asked looking at me like I'd lost my mind.

"I know that, baby, but I don't want to gamble with our kids future, especially when we don't even know if I'm gonna be good at this shit. I don't want to taint the well of wealth that your family worked hard to establish," I stated.

"Okay, so why don't you just use the money that's in the off shore accounts, I mean that's what my dad used for his risky business ventures, and trust me it paid off *handsomely*."

"You mentioned something about money in the islands and in Switzerland, but, baby, I don't know anything about it nor do I have access," I said.

"Sweetheart, we can fix that as soon as we get home. *Always* come to your wife first, especially when it comes to money because my father raised me like one of the Rothschild's, meaning we don't let outsiders get involved without money."

"Okay," I replied slowly, acting as if I had no idea of who she was talking about.

Her reference to the old Jewish family that single handily invented the concept of secure banking, no outsiders ever, and family first, gave me a peek at a side of her that I didn't know about.

She was more than just a crazy, white girl who liked to get fucked, and she talked about business like she'd learned a lot from dear old dad. Almost made me wonder why she killed him. One thing I know for certain was I couldn't go at this business thing half cooked because I needed to know what my wife knew.

Luckily, for me she was eager to tell me more, and we kept up our conversation through the preparation of early dinner and into the meal. Since it was still daylight, I decided to put her in the car and go sightseeing. Of course, she'd been to Puerto Rico before, and since I hadn't, she became my official tour guide. We did a little shopping, got some ice cream and made it back to the villa in time to watch the beautiful sunset from the balcony. Not surprisingly this took place with me pounding dick into her from the back while I thought of Amee and wondered where she was.

Just as Katrina suggested we take our next round down to the beach my phone started ringing, and I answered it without thinking because I needed to hear Amee's voice.

"Mr. Monroe, its Tobias Fraisure."

"You must be burning the midnight oil," I said, getting an uneasy feeling.

"Yeah, and it's a good thing because I just got some information. You're not gonna like it."

"Lay it on me," I said, stepping away from Katrina.

"Ira is getting ready to be indicted for murder and extortion. Thanks to your wife."

Chapter 13
4 days later

"Hey, fat man!" I said excitedly, picking my son up and holding him over my head.

His immediate smile and giggles melted my heart, bringing a sense of peace that had eluded me since my last moment spent with Amee. Shit had truly been a downward spiral since then, but I blocked all of that from my mind and focused on the adorable blessing I was holding.

"Did you miss me? Huh? Did you miss your daddy?" I asked, kissing his chubby little cheeks, much to his delight.

It didn't matter that he couldn't talk to answer my questions because the joy in his eyes said everything that I ever wanted to hear.

"You're gonna hang with daddy today, so let's get you dressed," I said, laying him on his changing table.

Once I had a fresh diaper on him, I dressed him in an all-white linen Gucci short set, and popped his pacifier in his mouth to keep him occupied while I packed his diaper bag. I'd already informed the nanny to make his bottles which I would pick up on our way out.

"Come on, stinker," I said, picking him up.

"Ahmani, we need to talk."

I turned around to find Katrina standing in the bedroom doorway, and just the sight of her was threatening to kill my vibe.

"Now you wanna talk?" I asked sarcastically.

"I tried to talk to you the whole time we were in Puerto Rico, but you either ignored me or screamed at me."

"Can you blame me? You did some foul ass shit Katrina, and you act like you can't see that," I said, trying to keep my voice calm so I wouldn't upset Little Ahmani.

"I made a decision that was best for our *family*, Ahmani, or do you think that Ira's freedom is more important than mine?"

"Don't give me that shit because you had plenty of other strategies to use to defend yourself in court, but you *chose* to do some sucka shit," I replied, putting my son in his carrier and buckling him in.

"All the strategies in the world are *not* guaranties, Ahmani! What if the jury would've decided that me taking a life was wrong no matter what, and that I deserved to go to prison? Would you have been okay with our kids losing their mother? Would you have been okay losing me?"

Never before had the truth wanted so badly to come out of my mouth, but it would cost me more than ever if I exposed my hand now. The web of deception that I was living in was getting more tangled and complex, but there was still a way for me not to become this black widow's dinner. I just had to stay focused.

"Like I told you in Puerto Rico, you should've come and talked to me instead of being on some sneaky shit with your lawyer," I said, grabbing my son and his diaper bag.

For a moment, she stood there blocking the doorway, but the look I gave her quickly conveyed my willingness to beat her mufuckin' ass today if she tested me, so she moved.

After adding Ahmani's bottles, extra formula and food to the bag, I strapped him into the back of the Hummer and left.

I didn't exactly know where I was going, I just needed time to think without Katrina sucking up all the air around me. It had almost made me physically sick to stay in Puerto Rico with her for three more days after Tobias' phone call, but Amee's words about doing what was best for her and the kids played over and over in my mind. I'd had to give her time to make it back to the DMV, but it was *hard* not to kill Katrina.

130

When Tobias had told me Black Boy was gonna be indicted, because of my wife, I didn't see how that was even possible, so anger wasn't my first reaction. But when he'd told me about her sworn statement that Black Boy had admitted to the killing, and demanded half a million dollars while threatening to implicate *me* on the murder, I was beyond pissed! It wasn't like this was some spur of the moment shit or a play to help her out of her legal troubles either, because I believed she always intended to out Black Boy out of my life. He was loyal, and he was a killer, which made Katrina more than nervous.

It didn't make her stupid, though. She *knew* I would've never agreed to her fuckery, and I damn sure wouldn't have made a statement against Black Boy. That was precisely why she'd convinced me to go out of town while her lawyer got a grand jury convened, and she gave her testimony. She'd made sure to explain my reluctance to make a statement or testify as fear because of what had happened to my family, and of course they bought that.

The bitch was truly more masterful at playing puppet master than Gepeto! And because my sole focus had been on Amee, I hadn't seen any of this coming!

"Your grandma warned me about thinking with my dick," I said, looking at my son in the rear-view mirror.

Of course, his response was that huge grin as he kicked his little legs. I thought my drive had been void of a destination, but forty-five minutes later, I was pulling up in front of the Prince William county jail.

"Come on, fat man, let's go see your crazy ass godfather," I said, getting out of the truck.

After making sure to bring an extra diaper, wipes, and a bottle, we went in. Thankfully, we didn't have to wait that long to get upstairs or for Black Boy to be called out, but I could tell by the look on his face that he hadn't expected to see me.

"I thought it was time that you met your godson," I said, once he picked up the phone.

"He's got Elyse's eyes, but he definitely looks like you. Let's just hope he's *smarter* than you."

"Bruh, I did *not* see this coming," I said.

"Ahmani, I *told you* it was coming! I told you based on the questions they were asking that I was getting a bad vibe, but you didn't listen, my nigga."

"I *did* listen, though, and I went fishing, too, but I'm telling you that those cards were held closer than Vegas. She had to play it like that because you know that I *never* would've went for no shit like that," I stated genuinely.

"Yeah, I know. The question is what the fuck do we do now?" He asked, looking at me closely.

"Now, we gotta stall for time, bruh. The babies are due in three months, after that you know what it is."

"I can do a few months, but are you sure that you can? I know that you didn't keep quiet about your conversation with Tobias because he heard you call her a bitch before you hung up," he said.

"It got ugly for sure, but it's all good. Me not saying anything to her would've been more suspicious because she knows that I'm the one dealing with your lawyer. She knew that shit was gonna hit the fan, but as long as her deal was in place, she wasn't worried."

I could see the fury in his eyes, and I sympathized with him. The fact that he was in this situation only added to the guilt I'd been carrying since my family was killed because now, he was another person affected by my decision to fuck with Katrina. She really was the gift that kept on giving.

"Have you talked to Amee?" I asked, switching subjects.

"Nah, have you?"

I hesitated before speaking, trying to decide exactly what I was supposed to tell him.

"If you're thinking about bullshitting me, don't bother. What's going on?" he asked.

"She's pregnant."

"By who?" he asked quickly.

When I just looked at him, he started laughing like this was the funniest shit he'd ever heard in his life, which of course got my sons attention and had him smiling.

"Glad you think it's funny," I said.

"My godson does, too."

"Can you be serious, nigga, this is real life," I said impatiently.

"A'ight, my bad. I thought Amee couldn't have no more kids though."

"Yeah, apparently she thought the same thing which is why the topic of birth control never came up," I replied.

"Damn, my nigga, so you about to have four kids under the age of one?" he asked, laughing again.

"Fuck you, Ira."

"Okay, no more laughing at your pain. How's Amee doing?" he asked seriously.

"I don't know, we haven't talked in a few days."

"Well, where is she?" he asked.

"She was in Puerto Rico, but I…"

"Puerto Rico? And you took that crazy ass bitch Katrina down there," he said, angrily.

"Calm down, nigga. I went down there first and that's when I found out about Amee being pregnant. We agreed that once Katrina got to Puerto Rico that Amee and Isaiah would leave, and go to Maryland."

"Ahmani, you're playing a dangerous game with deadly consequences, and you've already underestimated your wife too many times. You gotta be smart about this shit."

"I know that, bruh. That's why I told Amee the truth about everything," I replied.

"Ooh, how hard did she hit you?"

"Man, that little woman hits like a grown ass nigga!" I said, running my chin at the memory of her punch.

I didn't get mad when he laughed at me this time, I just joined in with him and my son.

"So, where does that leave you two?" he asked.

"I love her, I always have on some level."

"And now she done put that good good on you, and got you open," he stated, smiling.

"Oh, it goes both ways, you better know *that*. You already know that everything about my relationship with Amee is different and its built to last, but first I gotta deal with the other woman in my life. Without underestimating her this time."

"I trust you to handle everything, and what you can't handle I'm sure Tobias can," he said.

"He told me the cops have searched everywhere they can think of for that five hundred thousand dollars, they even took your car apart like it was a Lego set," I said, chuckling.

"Guess they need to check their sources more thoroughly. Tell Amee I love her, and congratulations."

"I will," I replied, standing up to leave.

I put Little Ahmani's carrier in the window and put the phone to his ear so his godfather could say a few words to him before we left. Once we'd made it back to the truck, I text Amee, hoping that she would respond to me instead of giving me the silent treatment like the past few days. I was just about to give up and pull off when my phone rang.

"Hey, baby," I said cautiously.

"Hi. I'm sorry I was ignoring you, but I wasn't feeling good. I had one of my flare ups."

"You okay, Amee?" I was concerned.

"I'm good now, but I'm already missing the warm weather of Puerto Rico. That's for damn sure."

"Where are you?" I asked.

"Why?"

"Was that a serious question sweetheart," I replied patiently.

"Yeah. Why do you wanna know where I am?" she asked.

"Because I wanna see you, and you should already know that."

"I'm not sure what I know, Ahmani, or what you want me to know," she said.

"You know that I love you. You know that nothing can or will change my love for you or the friendship we have."

"The fact that I'm pregnant changes *all* that, especially if you turn out to be like your cousin with his trifling ass. I..."

"Whoa, hold up, slim, you know that I ain't never *been* nor will I ever *be* like your other baby daddy, or any nigga you've been in a relationship with, so don't even go there," I stated quickly.

"All men say they're different until they're put to the test."

"Put me to the test, then," I challenged.

"I ain't got time for all that, Ahmani, you just need to prove yourself."

"But, baby, how can I do that if you won't even tell me where you are?" I reasoned softly.

For a while she didn't say anything. And then the silence was interrupted by an incoming text message. When I read it I smiled.

"I'm on my way. I love you," I said.

"I love you, too, even though you make me sick," she replied, laughing as she hung up.

I laughed too which of course got Little Ahmani's attention.

"What do you say, fat man, you wanna go visit your step mama?" I asked, propping his bottle so that he could eat while I drove.

Once I had him situated, I got us on the move. It only took me a little over an hour to get to the Ramada Inn motel that her and Isaiah were staying at, and I stopped to pick up some Chinese food along the way. When she opened the door, I handed her the food while I went to get my sleeping fat baby out of the truck.

"He's so cute," Amee whispered, immediately taking the carrier from my hand.

I could tell where her primary focus was gonna be for a while.

"What's up, Isaiah?" I asked, giving him a hug.

"Nothing much, just playing Grand Theft Auto 5," he replied, going right back to the PlayStation portable 4 in his hands.

"Pause it so you can get some of this Chinese food while it's still hot," I said, unpacking the food on the table.

After he made his plate, I fixed Amee a plate of beef and broccoli, and took it to her.

"You think your ass is slick, don't you?" she asked, accepting the food with a smile.

"I don't know *what* you're talking about."

"Yes, you do, nigga. First you show up on my doorstep with this adorable baby, and then you bring me the food that you *know* I constantly craved while I was pregnant with that big head boy over there," she said.

"I *don't* have a big head mom, and if I do, I got it from you."

Isaiah and I both laughed while Amee gave us the evil eye.

"Little Amee, this was not some diabolical plan on my part. I had Junior with me because I took him to see his god-father, and I couldn't just show up on your doorstep empty handed because that very impolite."

"Don't try to come at me with that old fake ass logic, boy, you know your sneaky ass is up to no good," she insisted.

"Isaiah, is your mom always this suspicious?" I asked.

"More like paranoid," he replied, earning him the pillow that she hurled at him and causing us both to laugh.

"So, what's going on with Black Boy?" Amee asked.

That question had a sobering affect real quick, but I knew that I couldn't lie to her.

"Isaiah, keep an eye on your cousin while we step outside for a minute," I said, taking Amee by the hand and leading her out to the truck.

The fact that she brought her plate with her didn't escape my notice, but now wasn't the time for me to crack anymore jokes.

"There's a lot to catch you up on, and you're not gonna like any of it," I warned, once we were seated in the truck.

"Don't sugar coat it, keep it one hundred."

I ran everything down to her form Puerto Rico to now without leaving out any detail, and she took it all in without a question, chewing her food thoughtfully. When I was done talking, she simply shook her head and looked over at me.

"No pussy in the world should be that good that you didn't see this level of crazy in that bitch. I mean, every woman has a little crazy in her, but, Ahmani, *this* bitch had an entire con-tinent of crazy in her!"

"The intelligence hides the crazy and that how I didn't see it, but I'm well aware of it now," I replied.

"So, what's your plan?"

"It's simple, I'm gonna leave her ass with absolutely nothing and no one because that's worse than death to her. I don't think that she's scared of dying, but being alone with no one to love her is what keeps that bitch up at night," I said.

"I hope you know what you're doing."

"Do you trust me?" I asked.

"God help me, but yeah I trust your tender dick ass."

"Then don't worry because I'm gonna take care of everything," I promised, leaning over and kissing her gently.

"You're not getting no pussy, Ahmani."

"Now see, I wasn't even on that today," I replied laughing.

"*Sure*, you weren't."

"On some real shit, Amee, I just came to kick it with you and let you spend some time with your stepson. I even brought you a gift."

"Oh, yeah, what's that?" she asked, looking at me warily.

I lifted up the armrest, pulled out the .40 Desert Eagle, and handed it to her.

"I know I don't have time to teach you all the tricks I learned, but I'm sure that you know how to point and shoot. At least this way you're not riding around naked and vulnerable."

"I appreciate that, baby," she replied, kissing me again quickly before inspecting the gun further.

"You can carry it inside this," I said, grabbing the diaper bag from the backseat, and passing it to her.

After looking at it for a while longer, she put it in the bag and opened the door to get out of the truck. I was about to follow her lead when my phone rung. I didn't know the number, but I answered anyway.

138

"Is this Ahmani Monroe?"

"Yes," I replied slowly.

"I'm calling from Fairfax Janova hospital where your wife Katrina Monroe was just admitted. She's been in a car accident, please hurry."

Aryanna

Chapter 14

"My wife, Katrina Monroe," I said, breathless from my sprint from the parking lot.

The nurse behind the desk immediately put her fingers to work for me.

"Emergency room two," she replied, pointing me down the hall.

It only took me seconds to get where she told me to go, finding Katrina bruised and cut up laying in a hospital bed. Her eyes were closed, but I couldn't tell if she was sleep or not. I just knew that she had to be in pain.

"Bae," I said, my voice cracking with emotion as I moved toward her.

She didn't open her eyes or respond in any way that indicated that she'd heard me, but I could tell by looking at the machines that she was hooked up to that she was alive. Based on the way her hospital gown fit her she was still pregnant too. I took a seat by her bed and took her hand in mine, unsure of what to say or feel in this moment. The hate that I felt for her was always just below the surface, but knowing that she was carrying my children always caused an internal struggle. In a moment like this it was impossible for me to emotionally separate the three of them, and I was left asking myself what would happen if they died or if she did.

"Are you her husband?" a tall, attractive blonde lady in a white lab coat asked this question, but I didn't know who she was or where she came from.

"Yes, I am, I'm Ahmani Monroe."

"Mr. Monroe my name is doctor Amelia Black, we spoke on the phone," she said, extending her hand.

"How bad is it? Are my babies okay?"

"The children are fine, they don't seem to be distressed, but we're gonna be monitoring them closely. As for your wife, she was incredibly lucky to come away with some cuts and scrapes, and a broken wrist. She'd unconscious, and I don't know how long she'll be that way, but her brain function is not abnormal," she replied.

"If her brain function is normal, then why isn't she waking up?"

"Honestly, I don't know the answer to that. The brain is much more complicated than the wonders of modern medicine would have you believe, so there's a lot we don't know. All we can do is watch and wait. I'll be ordering a new cat scan every four hours for the next twenty-four hours just to make sure I'm monitoring her brain wave patterns," she replied.

"Do you know what happened?" I asked.

My question put a different look in her eyes that I didn't understand.

"Well, from what I was told your wife plowed through a guard rail and clipped a tree."

"Which car was she driving?" I asked.

"I believe the rescue workers said that it was a silver Porsche, what was left of it anyway."

The guilt I felt was instant because I now knew Katrina had gone driving because she was frustrated, and she was frustrated because of how I'd been treating her.

"She must've lost control of the car," I said softy.

"Mr. Monroe, does your wife have any history of mental illness or depression?"

It took everything in me not to laugh out loud or make a scathing comment, but I managed to keep my composure.

"No," I replied shortly.

"Is this her first pregnancy?"

"Yes, but we have another son who's a couple months old," I replied.

"Was she looking forward to expanding your family, or did she seem overwhelmed?"

"She was excited, especially because we just found out last month that she was having twins. I could be misreading this doctor, but those don't seem like the typical questions asked upon admission to the hospital for a car accident," I said, looking at the doctor closely.

"You're right, and they aren't routine questions, but the rescue worker had some concerns. The car she was driving is nothing more than an expensive soda can now, but the concerns arise from the fact that there were no fresh skid marks."

I let her statement hang in the air as I watched the steady rise and fall of Katrina's chest and abdomen. I knew what she was implying, and I knew Katrina was capable of unspeakable horrors, but not even she would go that far.

"My wife didn't try to kill herself and our unborn children," I stated confidently.

"I pray that's not the case, Mr. Monroe, but I will warn you that she will have to see a different kind of doctor before she's discharged and released."

"I understand," I replied.

"Okay. Well, she should be moved to a private room shortly, and I can have a cot put in there if you wish to spend the night by her side."

"I would appreciate that very much Dr. Black."

"No problem, I'll see you again in a little while," she replied, leaving the room.

I sat in silence and observed Katrina's quiet beauty, wondering how she'd come to be so ugly inside. True enough, she had demons just like the rest of the world, but she had more opportunities than the average person, so her life's good should've easily outweighed the bad. If I only knew the beauty that was on display, I would shout down god himself if he accused her of wrong doing, but unfortunately I knew the darkness that had stained her soul. Even if I couldn't kill her because some part of me acknowledged that she needed serious help, I still couldn't allow her to infect my children. I could let her steal their innocence like she had Kendrick's and Keisha's. So, then what was I gonna do? What was I prepared to do, and was there really such a thing as going too far?

"We've come too far to turn back now bae, so don't you even *think* about dying," I said, squeezing her hand before bringing it to my lips, and kissing it.

"Mr. Monroe, we need to take her for another cat scan, and then we're moving her upstairs," a short brunette said, from the doorway.

"What room will she be in?"

"Room 424," she replied.

I stood up and kissed Katrina on the forehead before moving out of the way so that she could be wheeled out. I knew that time was of the essence so I headed to my truck and got on the move.

My first call was to Tobias Fraisure, quickly telling him what I needed done, and agreeing to pick it up from his office in an hour. Next, I called Amee and let her know what was going on. I wanted to tell her the plan that was formulating in my mind, but I realized that it was best to keep her on the sideline for the moment.

Instead, I asked her to keep Little Ahmani for me until I knew exactly what was going on with Katrina, and of course she agreed. With that taken care of, the only thing that I really needed to do next was a little bit of shopping for some essential items to bring my plan together.

By the time I finished shopping, it was time to meet up with Black Boy's lawyer so I drove directly to his office in downtown Manassas.

"I appreciate you seeing me on such short notice," I said, taking a seat in front of his desk.

"Are you some type of legal trouble, Mr. Monroe?"

"Call me, Ahmani, and no I'm not. Were you able to draft the document that I requested?" I asked.

"Yeah, I got it right here, but me doing that ain't worth ten thousand dollars," I said.

I ran down my plan to him, admitting that I was free-styling some parts because the pieces of the puzzle were still coming together. I was confident in it nonetheless though, and by the time I'd finished talking I could tell by the look in his eyes that he shared my belief in the outcome if everything was properly executed.

"You understand that you can't tell Ira, right?" I asked.

"I'm bound to you by attorney-client privilege."

We shook hands, and I made my exit. Despite wanting to go straight back to the hospital I decided to go home and get a few things to make Katrina's room homier. I made sure to pack a bag of clothes for both us, and then I was right back out the door and on the road. Since I didn't get a bite of Chinese food, I figured that I'd grab some of that good barbecue, and thankfully the waitress who'd given me her number wasn't there because I wasn't in the mood. I finally made it back to the hospital and up to Katrina's room feeling like I'd did a triathlon with absolutely *no training*. Before I got comfortable with my food, I put things in order around the room. I'd brought some pictures of the two of us, and some with us and Ahmani Junior. I'd brought the comforter from our bed, which I covered her up with, and I brought her favorite slippers.

"I know you smell this good food with your hungry ass, but I'm not about to try to feed you in your sleep. I learned my lesson the last time I tried to put meat in your mouth while you were sleep, so you better wake up," I said, chuckling as I opened up my first container of food.

When she still didn't stir, I ran a rib across her lips, leaving a trail of barbecue sauce, and expecting her tongue to shoot out like a lizard that spotted a fly. She didn't move though.

"Oh yeah, you really are unconscious," I said, eating my food.

By the time I got through the first rack of ribs, fries, and biscuits, my eyelids were hanging like curtains and the cot that the doctor had set up was looking like a water bed. I maneuvered it so that I'd be sleeping beside Katrina and not in the way of whoever came in to check on her during the night. As soon as my body went horizontal, I was sound asleep, and I didn't wake up again until they had to come get her for the next cat scan of course I couldn't go so I went back to sleep.

A little after sunrise, I got up and ate my second tray of ribs, knowing that cold barbecue was better than warm hospital food any day of the week.

"You're killing my staff with your food selection," doctor Black said, smiling as she walked into the room. "They don't like barbecue?"

"On the contrary, every nurse on this floor *swears* by the food from Memphis BBQ so they knew what you had sight unseen," she replied chuckling.

"The food *is* amazing, and I figured that since Katrina loves it, and my unborn kids swear by it, that I'd bring some with me. Trust me, when she didn't wake up for this, I knew that shit was real."

"Well, I suggest that you either save her some or get rid of the evidence because she could wake up anytime," doctor Black replied.

I pointed toward the five full Styrofoam trays behind me, making her chuckle again.

"When do you think she'll wake up?" I asked.

"I can't give you a specific time because then you'll hold me to it, but there's nothing neurological that's preventing her from waking up. Her brain is in a state of rest, and her eye flickers indicate that she's dreaming. I know it's frustrating, but honestly your wife won't wake up until she's ready to."

"Frustrating isn't a big enough *word* for this waiting game, but I know that there's nothing else I can do," I said.

"Adding touches of home and bringing things around that are familiar to your wife are good steps to take. So is talking to her like it was any other day, you know just natural flowing conversation."

"Knowing her that'll definitely wake her up because she loves to get the last word," I replied laughing.

"It's our right as women to get the last word, and a smart man wouldn't argue with that."

I put my hand straight in the air signifying my intelligence, which made her laugh.

"I'll be back to make my rounds in a couple hours. Do yo want to bathe your wife or would you rather one of the nurses do it?" she asked.

"I can handle it."

"Okay, you'll find everything you need in the bathroom, and make sure you pull the curtain for privacy because the door doesn't have a lock," she said, leaving us alone.

I wanted to finish my breakfast, but it made more sense to get her bath out of the way before the hospital started buzzing with activity.

After closing the door, I went to the bathroom and filled her pink foot tub with hot water, making sure to add her body gel that I'd brought from home. I carried that and her loofa to the table that was there for her food, closed the curtain around us, and pulled the blankets from around her so I could undress her. It wasn't until I had her naked that I had the best worst idea.

"The doctor *did* say that familiarity was a good thing," I said, smiling wickedly.

I watched her face closely as I put my hand in between her thighs, gently pushing two fingers inside her pussy.

"Damn, even *unconscious* you're wet," I said, shaking my head in amazement.

Despite my skilled fingers, I didn't see so much as a twitch come over her face. Her pussy did get wetter though.

"Ahmani!" she gasped suddenly, clenching my arm with her good arm.

I'd hoped that this would be the end result, but the way she came back from the dead startled me so bad that I feared my heart would stop.

"It's okay, Katrina, it's me, it's me, baby," I said, holding her close.

"What are you doing? Why am I naked in a hospital bed?"

"You don't remember what happened?" I asked, turning her to face me.

She shook her head slowly for a second, but then I saw the light of memory dawn in her eyes.

"I was in a car accident, wasn't I?"

"Yeah, you were, and you turned my Porsche into a soda can," I said smiling.

"Oh, my God, the babies!" she exclaimed panicked, grabbing her stomach.

"Relax, sweetheart, the babies are fine and you only have some cuts, bruises, and a broken wrist."

"Thank God! It could've been so much worse, bae I was *so scared*," she said emotionally.

"Baby, what happened?"

"I went for a drive, you know, to try and get over us fighting. I was distracted and I took the off ramp to fast, and when I tried to hit the brake, I hit the gas instead," she replied, ashamed.

"That explains why there were no skid marks. Do you know they actually asked me if you would've crashed the car on purpose trying to kill yourself, and the kids?"

"I would *never* do no shit like that!" she replied, vehemently.

"Baby, *I* know that. I mean I know that you're crazy and you'll go to extremes, but that's too far even for you."

"Why would you say that I'm crazy and an extremist?" She asked.

"Because I know you, Katrina."

"Maybe you only *think* you know me. Maybe you have no idea who I am," she said, smiling.

"Baby, I know you better than anyone in the *world* knows you. I know your thoughts, I even know your secrets."

"I don't have any secrets," she replied hesitantly.

I laughed at the expression on her face, which only served to annoy her.

"Why are you laughing, I *don't* have secrets, Ahmani."

"Of course you do, bae, but it's okay because I remember."

"You remember what?" she asked quickly.

"*Everything*."

Aryanna

Chapter 15

"You remember everything," she said slowly, searching my face intently.

"I do."

"Are these phantom memories based on conversations you've had with people because."

"Nobody would be able to describe the feeling of you giving me head the first night I got out of the jail, the sensations from the heat of your mouth mixed with the freezing milkshake on your tongue," I said smiling.

I wasn't surprised when she didn't smile back because I could see the fear that was bordering on terror in her eyes.

"Relax, sweetheart," I said, kissing her lips gently before climbing out of the bed.

"I was just about to give you a sponge bath, or do you feel up to a shower?" I asked.

"I'll take a shower later. I think we-we need to talk," she replied shakily.

"About?"

"Bae, if you remember everything then you know that there's *a lot* we need to talk about," she said.

I sat down in the chair next to her bed, and pulled the papers I'd had Tobias draw up out of my bag.

"Do you wanna have a real conversation, no lies, and no games?" I asked.

When she nodded her head yes, I turned the papers I was holding around so that she could see exactly what they were.

"You want a divorce?" she asked weakly.

"That was my initial reaction, and I'm sure you can understand that. I mean, you killed my mother, Elyse, Kendrick and Keisha."

"Ahmani, please I..."

"Then, I asked myself why you did what you did? Were you really just that horrible of a person, that *evil* at your core? The strange thing is that even knowing what I know it was hard for me to draw that conclusion because through all of this you did one thing that went against your norm. You spared my son. I *know* that you could've killed him, and you undoubtedly would've found some way to get away with it, but you didn't kill him. You loved him, instead. Then you did something else that went against the character of an evil person, you stayed by my side at the hospital. There was *no way* for you to know what I would say when I woke up, or what I would remember. So, the only explanation for you being there was because you loved me and…"

"Ahmani, I *do* love you. I swear to God on our kids that I love you!" she said passionately, crying steadily.

"I know that bae, that's the point I'm getting to. If it hadn't been for Kendrick and Keisha getting killed, I would believe everything you did was out of love, and because you didn't want anyone to come between us. My mom didn't like you, but hell, she barely liked me. And Elyse, well it's obvious why you wanted her out of the way…but my brother and sister were *innocent* and-."

"Baby, he wasn't supposed to shoot your brother and sister!" she said, shaking her head vigorously.

"What are you saying, Katrina?"

"I'm saying that when I contracted the shooter it was *only* for your mom, but I fucked up by being impatient and ordering a rush job. I *never ever* meant for your brother and sister to die, and that's why I offered up half a million for the shooter," she replied.

"But you could've simply told Black Boy where the shooter was since you were the one that hired him, *if* you were serious about making it right."

"Nobody knew where the muthafucka was, though, bae! Killing your brother and sister spooked him so he vanished. I *still* don't know how he was found," she said.

"You mean Ira didn't tell you that when he confessed to you?" I asked sarcastically.

"Ahmani, you know why I told that lie, plus you know that he doesn't want us together."

My silence acknowledged the truth in the statement she made, and gave me time to choose my next words carefully.

"I don't know why people don't want to see us together, but bae you should've always known that nobody would ever decide that except us," I said.

"And now you're deciding to divorce me, and leave me like everyone else?" she asked, crying harder.

I could see the agony on her face, and despite the compassion I knew I was projecting I was smiling happily inside. I let the silence drag on until I thought she was about to walk face first into hysteria, and then I continued.

"Katrina, you love me, right?"

"Yes."

"Any you love our babies, right?" I persisted.

"Yes, of course."

"Okay," I said simply.

It took her a few moments to get herself back under control, but she never took her eyes off of me.

"Okay. What?" she asked.

I slowly held up the divorce paper for her to see and then I ripped them in half.

"You mean it, Ahmani?"

I put the papers in my bag and, I climbed back in bed with her, pulling her close to me.

"You see that picture of you, me, and Ahmani Junior," I said, pointing to one of the few that was on the shelf directly above our heads.

"Mmhmm."

"That picture symbolizes what's important, bae. *Family*, our family, and I want to keep that together. If that's still what you want," I said.

She immediately kissed me with a desperation that I'd never experienced from her, and it quickly manifested itself in other ways because she was suddenly on top of me.

"Katrina, we're not done talking yet..."

"We are for now," she replied, using her good hand to free my dick so that she could imprison it inside of her.

"You owe me an apology," I said, grabbing her hips to try and hold her steady.

"I'm so sorry, Ahmani. I'm sorry that I got your brother and sister killed, and even your mom because it all caused you unbearable pain. I never wanted that, and I promise never to cause you pain again."

"Remember that promise," I said.

"I'll swear it in blood," she replied, kissing me passionately as she began moving with determination.

No sooner had I given myself over to the pleasure she was creating, I heard the door open and we both froze.

"Mr. Monroe, its Dr. Black, I just wanted to make sure you got your wife decent because they'll be up to take her for another cat scan shortly."

"Uh, Dr. Black this is Katrina, can you put a hold on that cat scan because right now I'm in the process of being *decently* fucked, and my brain is telling me that this is sooo necessary."

I had to suppress my laughter, but the doctor let hers echo off of the walls, merrily.

"Well, alright, but as your doctor, I'm ordering that you get two orgasms, no exceptions," Dr. Black replied.

"God, bless you Doc," Katrina said, already moving again.

Fifteen minutes and three orgasms later, she collapsed in a sweaty heap on my chest, fighting for air as much as I was.

"We need to fight more often because making up is *amazing*," she said, breathlessly.

"You don't gotta twist my arm."

The smile on my face was actually a genuine one instead of the millions of fake ones I'd had to deliver for the last six months. The biggest and riskiest part of my plan had paid off, so now all I really had to do was be just a little more patient and everything would work out perfectly.

"I love you, Ahmani."

"And you have no idea how much I love you," I replied.

"Yes, I do. I know it's not easy to forgive the things that I did because they were really fucked up, but the fact that you can *understand* why I did them shows me how much you really love me."

"Bae, people search everyday of their life for a love that they would die for, but only the blessed ones find it. The ones who are *meant* to be together," I said.

"And that's absolutely us because I wouldn't just kill for you, Ahmani, I'd die for you."

"Promise?" I asked, before I could stop myself.

She leaned up off my chest so that she could look me directly in the eyes.

"Cross my heart," she said solemnly, using her finger to demonstrate.

This time when the door to her room opened Katrina reluctantly climbed off of me and pulled the comforter up to shield her nakedness, and I got out of the bed.

"Am I back to soon?" Dr. Black asked, from outside the curtain.

"No, Doc, you're good," I replied.

"Hospital rooms are only good for quickies," Katrina said sullenly.

When the doctor pulled the curtain back, she was chuckling and her eyes were dancing with laughter.

"I remember what it was like to be nineteen," Dr. Black stated.

"It's only fun because the dick is good," Katrina whispered.

"You're so embarrassing sometimes," I said, shaking my head and laughing.

"I am not. Doctor, will you please tell my husband that good dick is an *essential* part of life for a woman, especially at my age when most females are test driving every dick they can find."

"Mr. Monroe, your wife does have a point. However, from the sounds that I heard all the way down at the nurse's station I'm gonna need you to remember that you *were* just in a car accident, Mrs. Monroe."

I didn't laugh at what the doctor said, I laughed at the bright red flush that washed over Katrina.

"I tried to be quiet," Katrina replied, defensively.

"If that was you trying to be quiet then the dick deserves a better description than *good*. I thought that your husband bringing food in here had my staff distracted and craving, but the way you sounded had three nurses request early lunches so that they could go home!"

By now, I was laughing hard enough to have tears coming from my eyes, but I still saw where my wife's attention was.

"Food? You brought food? Wait, is that why I tasted barbecue sauce on my lips when I woke up?" she asked, looking at me.

"I may have brought some ribs to entice you out of your coma," I replied.

Katrina's eyes immediately went to the five trays taking up space on the window ledge, and I could tell that her mouth was watering something serious.

"Doc, I know it seems like I'm rushing you out every time you come in, but as you can see, I've still got business to handle so…"

"I understand, but I need you to come with me so we can take care of this cat scan. If you'll put your hospital gown on, I'll send a nurse in with a wheelchair," the doctor said.

"I can do that," Katrina said, grabbing her gown.

I waited until the doctor was gone before I dropped the news on Katrina that I knew she wouldn't like.

"Bae, I'ma make a few moves while you're getting you cat scan."

"What? Where are you going?" she asked, putting on her best sexy pout.

"I've got a few things to take care of before you get discharged, but don't worry I'll be back and I'll leave you one tray of this good food."

"*One* tray? Now you already *know* that's the wrong answer because I'm eating for three human beings, or don't you want our kids to be healthy?" She asked.

"That was a low blow, bae, you know my babies' health is my top priority."

"I'll show you a low blow later. For now, you just go handle your business as quickly as possible, and leave *all* those trays there because the doctor didn't mention shit about me being discharged," she said, putting her gown on and standing up.

A few seconds later, a nurse came in with a wheelchair and whisked her away so that they could have another look at her brain. If they knew what I knew, they'd stay out of that house of horrors. I quickly grabbed everything I needed from the room and then I was out the door.

Once I got in the truck, I sent Tobias a text letting him know that we were better than good, and I text Amee to let her know that I was on my way.

After making a stop at the bank, I went to the Verizon store and bought two new phones, then I jumped on the highway to see the woman that I loved beyond words. Of course, I picked up breakfast from McDonalds, and some flowers from a vendor working the motel entrance.

"I think you're trying to make me fat," Amee said, taking the flowers I offered when she opened the door.

I could tell by the flair of her nostrils that the egg McMuffins were calling her name, but I didn't say anything, I just stood there smiling.

"Stop grinning, fool," she said, smiling even though she was shaking her head.

She finally took the food from my hand and moved aside so that I could enter the room. I'd expected to find little Ahmani sleep and Isaiah playing his video game, but instead Isaiah had my son on the bed playing with him. The sound of his sweet baby laugh was such beautiful music to my ears.

"Hey, fat man," I said.

Immediately, his head and eyes began to swivel wildly, looking for me. When he finally spotted me, the grin on his face got even bigger and his eyes let up. His baby gibberish was coming out of his mouth a mile a minute, and the translation was: *nigga, where you been?*

"I guess somebody missed you," Amee said.

"Was he the only one?" I asked, looking at her as I moved toward Little Ahmani.

She didn't respond, but the smile on her face said enough.

"Isaiah, you better get some of that food before your mom inhales it," I warned.

"Fuck you, Ahamni," she said, causing us all to laugh.

While they ate, I gave my son the attention that he needed and wanted, and just enjoyed the carefree moments where his innocence was allowed to wash over me.

"I don't know how your son came out so good considering how bad your ass was as a kid," Amee said.

"Like you remember me at his age, girl please."

"Oh, you *know* I've heard all the stories about your spoiled ass nigga, so don't lie!" She said laughing.

"Just like I got all the stories on you little Amee, shall we rehash right here in front of our children?"

The look on her face said that I better not, so I kept my mouth shut and continued playing with my son.

"So, what's the deal with my sister wife and the kids?" She asked.

It was on the tip of my tongue to call her a bitch, but instead I looked at her hard enough to fuck up her edges.

"You're not *even* funny. The kids are fine, and Katrina finally woke up a little while ago."

"So, what happened?" she asked.

I ran the accident down to her, while conveniently leaving out exactly *how* Katrina woke up.

"Are you sure that she didn't do it on purpose?" Amee asked seriously.

"No," I admitted.

"Well, at least you're not being blind to the possibilities now."

"No, I'm not, I'm actually moving under the assumption that she *did* crash the car on purpose," I said.

"That sounds vaguely like you've come up with some hair-brained scheme since I last saw you."

"Isaiah-."

"I know, I know, watch this, baby," he replied, moving back to the bed I was on, but making sure to grab his food.

I signaled for Amee to follow me into the bathroom, and I turned on the shower once we were behind closed doors.

"You think my room is bugged or something?" she asked.

"No, I just need a shower and I figured we could talk while..."

"Why do you need a shower, Ahmani?"

This question came with the narrowing of these beautiful eyes, and I could see that the pilot light was definitely lit.

"Stay focused on what I'm about to tell you, please, because..."

"You fucked her, didn't you?" she accused, aggressively.

"If you will *listen,* I can explain why, Amee."

Despite the steadily building anger, she leaned against the sink and crossed her arms over her chest, allowing me time to speak. I ran the whole play down to her, knowing she would see the wisdom in the decisions I'd made. She let me talk uninterrupted for five minutes, but when I was done, she still didn't say shit.

"Well?" I asked, finally.

"You remember how you told me to put you and your love for me to the test?"

"Yeah," I replied, warily.

"Well, here's your test, don't fuck that bitch no more. Don't eat her pussy, don't let her suck your dick, you two need to live like roommates from now on."

"Amee, that's not realistic, you know that'll make her suspicious..."

"I don't give a damn *what* it makes her, Ahmani! According to you, you have everything you need so the only thing left to do is wait. You can go without fucking that bitch."

"Amee..."

"It's not negotiable, Ahmani. Now wash *my* dick off because I want some before you leave."

Aryanna

Chapter 16

"'Bout time you made it back, you've been gone for *hours*," Katrina said, clearly agitated.

"I'm sorry, bae, but somebody wanted to see you," I replied, holding Ahmani's carrier up for her to see him.

Her face immediately softened and her building anger was replaced by love.

"There's my little man," she cooed, pushing the necessary buttons to sit her bed up.

The sight of a familiar face had Little Ahmani squealing with delight as I sat the carrier in between Katrina's legs.

"I went home to take a shower and I figured that seeing our son would brighten your day."

"You always brighten my day, don't you handsome," she replied, giving him her hand to play with.

In actuality, I'd had to go home and take *another* shower because the one I'd taken in Amee's motel room had been pointless. Instead of her getting in the shower with me where I could've fucked her and still came out fresh. She'd waited until I'd finished showering and *then* fucked me. The icing on the cake was the fact that she demanded that I *didn't* take another shower, that I walk around smelling like her pussy the same way I'd done with Katrina's.

Needless to say, this demand was made while she was working me thoroughly, so I'd agreed without hesitation. I loved Amee, even when she was a bossy bitch, but what I *wasn't* about to do was provoke the crazy lady by coming around her. Smelling like another woman's pussy! Somehow that didn't seem like my smartest life decision.

"Oh, I know how to brighten your day, too," I said, holding up the shopping bag in my other hand for her to see.

"If your daddy is a smart man, then he has food in that bag," she said, smiling at my son, who was loving the attention he was getting.

"Bae, I didn't know that you wanted me to bring food, I mean I *did* leave five trays full of food here."

"So, are you calling me fat because I ate all that food, or because I'm still hungry?" She asked, smiling tightly.

I shook my head and laughed as I took a seat in the chair beside her bed.

"I'm too smart for you to walk me down that dark alley, sweetheart, plus you know how sexy you look pregnant."

"Mmhmm. What else I know is that you better have some food in that bag, especially because the doctor ain't releasing me today," she informed me.

"I kind of figured that she wouldn't since the reason that it took so long for you to wake up was unknown. It's okay though because your husband *knows* you," I replied, pulling the footlong meatball sub out of the bag, and passing it to her.

"Let this be your first lesson, Little Ahmani, your mommy *always* gets what she wants. Yes, I do."

I was smart enough not to contradict that statement, besides I was just happy to have avoided the attitude I'd known was awaiting my arrival. While she focused her attention on my son and the food in front of her, I was already back in my shopping bag pulling out another peace offering.

"Being that the doctor said the car was totaled I figured that that meant everything in it was lost, so I went and bought us new phones," I said, opening the first box to pull out the IPhone.

"That was thoughtful, bae. You got yourself a new one, too?"

"Yes, and before you say anything, I already know that you want me to set my security features so that your finger print can unlock my phone," I replied, plugging the phone charger into the wall socket.

She didn't even try to suppress her smile or deny that she'd been about to say that very thing to me, but it was okay because I was several steps ahead of her. Once I had both phones plugged in and charging, I pulled my own sub out of the bag, preparing to get down.

"Is that chicken and cheese?" Katrina asked longingly.

"Mind your business and stay over there."

"Babyyy," she whined.

"Not happening," I said, taking a huge bite while looking at her.

"Junior, your daddy is *so mean* sometimes."

The pout on her face made me laugh. I waited until we'd both finished our food before I revealed my last surprise of a six-inch steak and cheese, but I told her she couldn't have it until later.

After she fed Ahmani, I changed his diaper and put him to sleep, using the time to try and figure out how I wanted to have this next conversation.

"It's time for your cat scan, Mrs. Monroe," a nurse said, coming into the room with a wheelchair.

"This is getting annoying," Katrina replied.

"Bae, just go get it out of the way. We'll be here when you get back," I promised.

She reluctantly got out of bed and into the wheelchair, but she managed to blow me a kiss on her way out. Once she was gone, I pulled out my old phone and called Tobias.

"I'm about to activate our new phones," I informed him.

"Sounds like your plan is coming together nicely."

"Let's hope nothing else happens in the next few months," I said.

"As long as you play the dutiful and loving husband, everything should be fine. Just stay focused."

"I'll be in touch," I said, disconnecting the call.

I was tempted to call Amee, but the last thing I needed was for Katrina to catch me in the middle of that call, so I decided to text her instead. I kept it light be telling her that I missed her, but her response was to send me a picture of her pussy, telling me *that's* what I really missed. I was still laughing when the doctor suddenly appeared.

"Aww, he's so adorable," she whispered, going straight toward my son.

"He gets it from me."

The doctor looked around the room before turning her attention to me.

"I agree with that, but don't tell your wife," she whispered, winking at me.

I smiled at her in way that let her know that I knew she could get it, even though it wasn't smart to travel down that road.

"So, what's the deal, Dr. Black?"

"Well, the hold on your wife's release was about that chat I told you that she'd have to have with the psychologist, but I spent some time talking to Katrina earlier and she explained the accident. She appears to have all of her mental facilities and its clear how much she loves you and your children, so I spoke to the doctor myself. Your wife has officially been discharged and you can take her home," she concluded.

I smiled because I knew that she thought she was doing us a favor, but the reality was that Katrina could've benefitted from laying on those white folk's couch, discussing her life. Maybe even a couple sessions of electric shock therapy wouldn't hurt either.

"Thanks, Doc, I know that she'll be happy to hear that."

"Oh, I'm sure she will, especially because hospital rooms are only good for quickies," she replied, laughing.

I laughed with her, but then an idea hit me.

"Doc, she had trouble sleeping sometimes, and I know she needs her rest for the babies' sake. Is there anything that you can prescribe that won't harm the kids?"

"I mean I know of a few things, but she really needs to go see her primary care doctors, or her neonatal doctor," she replied.

"She's kinda proud, and sees insomnia as a weakness. Can't you just take care of it. Please?" I asked, smiling seductively.

The look she gave me told me that her panties had some added moisture in them, which was okay with me so long as it benefited my ultimate goal.

"You're very persuasive, Mr. Monroe," she stated softly.

"Trust me, you have *no* idea."

"Nothing comes free in this world, though, you know that, right?" she asked, smiling with mischievous intent.

"I'm aware of that."

Our suddenly seductive banter was reduced to nonverbal communication spoken through body language. I sized her up from head to toe, and she licked her lips.

I slowly unzipped my jeans, and she nodded her head slightly, while staring intently at the opening like we were at a magic show, and she was waiting for the big reveal. I had no loyalty to Katrina, so the question of whether or not to play this game with the doctor didn't factor her in. I didn't feel right cheating on Amee, though. True enough the medication I was trying to get out of the doctor would help me control Katrina by dictating her sleep schedule, and that would make more time for me and Amee.

I'd learned earlier that trying to use logic didn't work on Amee though. In the end I could only ask myself if my actions worked toward the greater good.

"Well, I can see what all the noise was about," Dr. Black said, hungrily eyeing the dick in my hand.

"It's been known to have that effect on people."

"I bet it has, so…"

"Dr. Black, are you looking for me?" Katrina asked, from behind her.

The expression on the doctor's face was too comical not to laugh, even as I was hurriedly shoving my dick back in my jeans before we got caught.

"Actually, I was," Dr. Black replied, turning to face Katrina.

"I hope you've come to tell me that you're going to stop checking my brain every five minutes because I'm starting to worry that I'll grow another head," Katrina said.

"Actually, I've got better news than that, you're being discharged and…"

"How soon?" Katrina quickly asked.

"Just as soon as you'll let me borrow your husband so we can get your paperwork done. We would've done it while you were getting your cat scan, but he insisted on being here when you got back."

"Baby, if there was ever a time, I would've given you a pass, now would be it. I want to go *home* and sleep in my own *bed*," Katrina replied, getting up out of the wheelchair.

"Okay, but that's gonna leave you with the task of getting dressed and packing up, can you handle that, Captain Hook?" I asked smiling.

"Keep acting like you don't know how capable I am with one arm, and its gone be a *long* night for you. Now will you please get me out of here," she said.

"Yes, ma'am. After you, Doc," I said, standing up and following her out of the room.

It looked like we were heading for the nurse's station, but suddenly she veered into a stairway, and we went up one flight. From there, she led me quickly to an office that had a desk in the middle of it, and a couch pushed up against a wall. The first thing that she did was go to her desk and start scribbling furiously on her prescription pad.

"Here you go," she said, extending me the slip of paper.

Before I could take it, she pulled it back, folded it, and stuck it in her bra.

"If you want it, come get it," she taunted.

My response was to unzip my pants and pull my dick out again.

"Right back at you."

She had her lab coat off, her pants and panties at her ankles, and was bent over the couch quicker than I could say Superman.

"Give it to me," she demanded seductively.

She may have been an older woman, but that old pussy felt like new pussy and I beat it up until a river of our cum mixture was running down her legs. Before she could collapse on the couch, I pulled the prescription out of her bra.

"Thank you, Doc."

"No, thank *you*," she replied emphatically.

"I know you'd love to lay there, but you've got paperwork to do."

"It's already done. You can take her home. Hell, you can take *both* of us home," she said seriously.

I chuckled as I stepped into her private bathroom and cleaned myself up. When I came back out, she was still sprawled on the couch, half naked staring at the ceiling, and I left her to whatever thoughts she was thinking.

By the time I made it back to Katrina's room, she was sitting on the bed messing with her new phone.

"You ready?" I asked.

"Everything is done already?"

"That's what happens when you have highly motivated people working for you," I replied, unhooking my phone from the charger, and putting everything back in my shopping bag.

"Can we stop for ice cream?" she asked smiling.

"Anything for you, bae."

I picked up my still sleeping son and led the way out to the truck. Once we were loaded up and, on the move, I felt like it was time to get back to the conversation I'd been preparing to have earlier before her cat scan.

"We need to talk about Black Boy," I said.

"What about him?"

"You need to recant your testimony bae, you know its bullshit," I replied.

"So, we're back to me gambling with my freedom again? I thought you loved me, Ahmani."

"Baby, I do love you, but…"

"No, no *buts*! If you love me, then you gotta ride for me whether I'm right *or* wrong because that's the only way that this relationship is gonna work. No one should *ever* come before me in your life, especially not someone who's destined for prison anyway. Don't you realize that if Ira actually had the control that he *thinks* he does then no one would've tried to carjack us in the first place? It's his fault I had to shoot a muthafucka!" she said passionately.

I actually had to look over at her to see if she was serious before I said anything because this bitch's logic was *whacked*!

"Are you seriously blaming the shit that happened on Black Boy?"

"Would you rather I blame you instead? I mean it *was* your idea for us to be in the ghetto in a one hundred-thousand-dollar car. You know maybe you should try being a little more grateful since I *did* save your life," she replied.

There were so many words that wanted to spew from my mouth that I had to literally keep my lips clamped shut and focus on driving. I didn't know if narcissistic was the right word to apply, but one thing that I know for damn sure was that this bitch was *absolutely* full of herself. Still, I knew that I had to press on.

"I just don't think that its right, bae, I mean I know how it feels to sit in jail when you're innocent," I said.

I knew my statement would address her question of whether or not she should blame me for the shooting because I could just as easily blame her for shit.

"Ira got caught with guns, Ahmani, he's not exactly innocent. But if it'll make you feel better, I'll give him some money, I think a million will cover his troubles."

"Not everything is for sell, Katrina."

The smirk she gave me and the chuckle that accompanied it were so condescending that I almost backhanded her in the face. I managed to fight the urge though.

"Just don't expect me to help," I said seriously.

"The thought never crossed my mind."

We rode the rest of the way home in complete silence, but I was good with that because I really wanted to choke the shit out of her. All I could do was keep telling myself to be patient over and over again.

When we got home, I took Little Ahmani upstairs, changed his diaper, and put him back to sleep in his crib. My plan had been to go down to the basement and fire a couple hundred rounds to relieve the stress that I was feeling, but I came out of the nursery to find Katrina waiting on me. With a gun in her hand.

"You forgot my ice cream," she said softly.

"I did."

"Would you mind going to get me some?" she asked.

"What kind would you like?"

"Cookies and Cream Cheesecake," she replied, smiling.

"I got you."

When I went to walk past her, she raised the gun, but quickly turned it around to hand it to me handle first.

"I know you probably haven't been carrying, but I want you to be safe at all times. This .45 will replace your other one that I had to use," she stated.

"Thank you."

When I grabbed the gun, she pulled me toward her and kissed me passionately. It wasn't until I'd pulled back that I noticed she'd pressed the barrel right to her heart.

"I love you, Ahmani, with all that I am and ever will be. If you don't feel the same way, just pull the trigger now, don't worry it's loaded and I won't feel but a moment of pain. That's better than a lifetime of living without you," she said emotionally.

To me the blue in her eyes symbolized her love, but the white around that symbolized the crazy. The combination was like ether and a match.

"I love you, Katrina, and you never have to doubt that," I said, kissing her again.

She stared deeply into my eyes before finally letting the gun go.

"Hurry back."

"I intend to," I replied, smiling.

I made my way downstairs to the truck and headed out. My first stop was the pharmacy so I could fill the prescription

I'd had worked hard for, and then it was off to Dairy Queen. I'd just put my order in for a gallon of ice cream when my phone rang.

"What's up, Tobias?"

"You were right, she already put the call in to find someone to handle Ira," he replied.

"A'ight, well, we already know how hard that's gonna be because of where he is, so we got time to…"

"Not as much time as you think. She wants to put a hit on Amee, too."

Aryanna

Chapter 17

"You look like shit," Tobias said, when I slumped into a chair in front of his desk at 7a.m.

"I didn't sleep well. Can you imagine why?"

"Oh, I know why, I'm just surprised that I'm actually seeing you in my office instead of having to come visit you at the jail because I thought for *sure* you were gonna kill her last night when I told you," he replied.

The truth was that I'd wanted to kill her. I'd wanted to watch her die in the most painful way possible, but I knew to do that meant killing my babies, and nothing could make me do that.

"For a while I thought the same thing. To tell you the truth I wasn't totally convinced that I wouldn't shoot her in her sleep when I left the house a little while ago," I said.

"Well, I'm glad that you didn't, but I hope you're here to tell me that you've got a plan."

"The plan to buy her a new phone, clone it, and put a bug in it seemed like a damn good plan, but now I don't know. I would've *sworn* that Amee was completely off her radar," I said, shaking my head in frustration.

"Undoubtedly, that's what she wanted you to think, but now you know what real is."

"Yeah, now I know that I gotta protect Amee and our unborn child from this crazy bitch!" I replied.

"Wait, Amee's pregnant, too? Now, this is some new age Jerry Springer shit."

"I'm glad I could amuse you, but can we stay focused please. I listened to the recording, and I don't feel like Katrina was specific enough," I said.

"I think that she was, I mean she made the call to someone in Chicago and said that she had two problems to get rid of.

175

Just because she didn't use the actual word *kill* doesn't mean that the inference can't be drawn."

"Okay, but is the tap legal?" I asked.

"If necessary, I can back channel it and have some friends make it legit. The other recordings that you've got are good though, as long as you have them in a safe place."

"Trust me they're safe," I replied.

"A'ight, well you just let me know what you wanna do and when you wanna do it."

"I need you to go sit down with Ira and tell him what's going on because it's not safe for him to be in the blind anymore," I said.

"I'll do it today. What's your next plan of action?"

"I'm gonna go try to talk some sense into Amee," I replied, standing up.

We shook hands and I left his office. I knew that I couldn't go straight to Amee now, but I sent her text to be expecting me sometime today.

With that done I made a quick stop at Krispy Kreme before heading back home.

"Hey, handsome, I was hoping you'd be back soon," Katrina said, when I came into the kitchen.

"Did you get my note?"

"I did, and I appreciate you being that thoughtful so I didn't wake up and panic," she replied, coming from around the counter to kiss me.

"I didn't want you in your feelings like last time."

"The only thing that I'm feeling is hungry and horny, but not necessarily in that order," she purred seductively.

"I'm all about multitasking bae."

Five minutes later, we were upstairs in bed with her riding my dick with a donut in her mouth. I wanted so bad to Facebook live this shit, but I knew she'd kill me. And if she didn't then Amee would.

A half dozen donuts and two monstrous climaxes later, I had completed my husbandly duties, and I was now free to proceed with my day. While Katrina was in the shower, I went down to the kitchen, setup the laptop, and started fixing me some breakfast.

"Damn, you got me hungry again. What are you doing?" she asked, fifteen minutes later when she walked into the kitchen.

"Like I told you earlier, bae, it's all about multitasking."

While I tended to my fried potatoes, she was looking at the computer screen with the available real estate classes I was looking into.

"Ah, I see that you were serious when we talked about this in Puerto Rico," she said, smiling.

"Of course, I was serious. I'ma be more than just your gigolo woman."

"But, baby, you're so good at it," she replied, laughing.

I stuck my tongue out at her, and that only made her laugh harder.

"Bae, what are you gonna do after you eat?" she asked.

"I figured I'd go look for something to replace my Porsche, why?"

"Because I'm gonna show you everything about those offshore accounts, so fix enough food for the both of us and meet me in my dad's study," she replied.

"Damn, how much can you eat?"

"Are we talking about pounds or inches?" she retorted, smiling wickedly.

"You're so *nasty*!"

"And you *love it!*" she sang, prancing from the room.

I quickly finished preparing the fried potatoes, bacon, eggs, and toast for both of us, and then I met up with her for my back to school session.

The first hour, I felt like I was trying to learn trigonometry and calculus, but by the second hour I was on my shit and confident about it too. I almost lost my mind when I saw that there was damn near two hundred million between these two accounts, but I played it cool.

"A'ight, so what I'm gonna do is set up a third account and move ten million into it, and that's what you'll start your investment with. Consider it the buy money, but you know you always gotta put the re-up money to the side first once you make your first sell," she said.

"Baby, you can teach me about offshore banking and how to hide money, but when it comes to the dope game, *I'm* the teacher and *you're* the student."

"Okay, *Tony Montana*," she replied smiling.

Once she had the new account set up, she gave me all three account numbers before shutting everything down.

"Go out into the world and multiple my son," she said, making the sign of the cross in front of me.

"Thank you, father," I replied, bowing.

We both laughed, but I could see her fighting off a yawn at the same time.

"You wanna go to the car dealership with me?" I asked.

"Ordinarily, I would love to, but I think your daughters and I are gonna take a nap."

"Okay, well I'll make sure to bring you some food back when I return," I said.

"You're the best husband in the world, Ahmani. You know what would really make me happy though?"

"What?" I asked.

"If you would hold me until I fell asleep."

I held out my hand to her, and when she took it, I led her back upstairs to our bedroom. I climbed in the bed first and then let her snuggle against me the way that she liked, but I knew this wouldn't last long. Sure enough within ten minutes she was snoring softly, and I was in the shower. I quickly got dressed, checked Little Ahmani, and then left the house.

My decision to take her 2015 Jeep Wrangler was a calculated one because I had a different destination in mind.

An hour later, I pulled up in front of the house that had effectively changed my life. Breaking into Katrina's house had put my life on a path that I could've *never* imagined possible, and the guilt that I carried was still so heavy that I had to take a minute before climbing out of the Jeep. Just like the first time I was here I was on a mission of survival, but the difference this time was that I knew information was the most valuable thing. Another big difference was that I now knew the passwords and the combinations to everything, which meant I wasn't blindly looking for shit. My first stop were the different safes spread throughout the house which contained the usual in the form of money and jewels, but also certificates of stocks that were owned.

"You didn't mention these, bae," I murmured to myself.

I quickly took pictures of everything before returning it to its original position. I was more surprised when I found nine passports, three a piece for mother, father, and daughter, all with different names and information on them.

"An escape plan," I marveled.

Once I had pictures of all of that, too, I put them back and moved on. When I was done with the bedroom and living room safes I went to her dad's study. My goal here was to learn what I could about his business because anyone who can generate half a billion dollars knows some tricks.

When I opened his safe, I found four different flash drives, and since pictures of these would do me no good, I decided to simply take them with me. It wasn't like I was stealing because I was in the family now. I felt like I'd gotten what I came for, and once I'd exchanged the Jeep for the all-white Bugatti Veyron I was back on the road.

My next stop was the bank, and then I was in the wind to see my Amee. I'd texted her from the bank to let her know that I was on my way since she hadn't responded to my text this morning. I didn't get her reply until I was about to get on the highway, and what she said made me stand on the brakes with both feet. Ignoring the blaring horns and angry rants of other drivers, I cut across five lanes of traffic and raced in the direction I'd just come from.

Fifteen minutes later, I was sliding to a stop in Georgetown south next to Amee's truck.

"Yo, what the fuck are you *doing* here?" I asked, hopping out the car, and moving toward where she was sitting on her front porch.

"Chill out, Ahmani, we were tired of being cooped up in the hotel so I decided to come home for the day."

"Amee, this is *not* your home anymore, and you know it ain't safe to be here!" I said angrily.

"We're safe, and this will *always* be my home," she replied, lifting the newspaper off the empty chair next to her to reveal the gun I'd given her.

"Having that don't make you safe, dummy, especially because this bitch had the means to buy way more than one gun or one shooter!"

"Don't call me out my fucking name, nigga, unless you want us to have a problem," she said, picking the pistol up.

"Like, I'm scared of you or something, bring your simple ass in the house," I demanded, walking past her and opening the front door to her spot.

Despite the dim lighting and the smell of stale air my mind still raced back to the last time I was in here. I knew that there was absolutely no time to focus on that, though.

"Nigga, you better stop talking to me like you don't know me," Amee said from behind me.

"You wanna have a civilized conversation? Cool, let's talk," I replied, turning around to face her.

"Ahmani it's no big deal…"

"Do you remember the conversation that we had in Puerto Rico? I'm talking about the one where you told me that I needed to do what was best for you and the kids, and not just me? So, was that some do as I say not as I do type shit?" I asked.

She didn't have a quick response to that question because she knew that not even the gun in her hand could justify her reckless actions.

"So, I'm supposed to just keep running from this bitch?" She finally asked.

"No, you're supposed to be mature enough to not see it as *running*, but as doing what's best for your children."

The flash of anger in her green eyes told me that she didn't like how I'd put that to her, but we both knew that I wasn't pulling no punches or taking back what I'd said.

"It's best for my child to have some type of normalcy in his life despite the bullshit that *you* dragged us into," she said.

"I can own my part in all of this, but let's not act like I *took* the pussy from you *or* intentionally got you pregnant. If we're playing the blame game trust me there's more than enough to go around."

"You're right you didn't take the pussy, but you damn sure *lied* to get it, didn't you?" she asked.

"So, me lying about my memory somehow absolves you from laying on your back and spreading your legs?"

"You know what, fuck you, Ahmani, I..."

"Raising that gun in my direction would be a mistake," I said calmly.

I could tell by the questioning look that she was giving me that she hadn't consciously realized her movements, but I'd peeped her body language.

"I wouldn't point a gun at you, Ahmani, you know that."

All I knew was what I'd seen, but there was no point in escalating an already heated argument.

"Baby, listen, you and the kids' safety is the most important thing to me because I can't lose you. I love you," I said, taking a step toward her.

She put the gun down on the table and pulled me toward her until our lips were doing the rest of the talking. Kissing her never got old, especially when her juicy lips held the promise of so much more.

"Do you have a problem if we make up here instead of back at the motel?" she asked seductively.

"That depends on if you would rather a long make up session or a short one."

"Well, Isaiah is at his cousins house which means we can definitely take our time here," she replied, already unbuttoning and unzipping my jeans.

"Mmm, sounds like..."

My words were interrupted by my ringing phone. I knew that there was no way Katrina should be awake by now because I'd crushed up two pills with her food, and one was good for four hours. Still, I pulled my phone out to check and when I saw who it was, I answered.

"Your timing *sucks,* my nigga," I said immediately.

"That must mean that you're with Amee," Black Boy replied.

"Yeah, and I was just about to wax…"

"Nigga, don't be telling my business, I don't know who that is," she said, punching me in the stomach.

"Hold on, bruh, I'ma put you on speaker phone," I said chuckling.

"You there, Black?"

"Yeah. And, Amee, that nigga ain't gotta tell me your business because I *seen* your business," he said, laughing.

"Fuck you, Ira," she said, laughing with us.

"It's too late to fuck me, you done chose that tender dick muthafucka over there. It's good to hear your voice though," he replied.

"It's good to hear your, too. How you holdin' up?" she asked.

"You know this shit ain't nothing to a real gangsta. What about you though, how you holding up" he asked.

"I'm good. I'd be better if this nigga over here wasn't always on my damn nerves," she replied, smiling at me.

"Slim, you know that nigga in *love* with you, so that means he gonna be on that extra shit."

"Why you muthafucka talking about me like I ain't standing here?" I asked.

"Because we don't give a fuck if you *is* standing there, chief tender dick," he replied laughing.

I could tell that Amee was trying to suppress her laughter, but she was doing a poor job of it.

"Black Boy, you should see the look on this nigga's face right now," she said.

"Tell the truth, Amee, you got him sprung, don't you?"

"I don't know if that's what you call it, but the nigga is definitely on one. If you would've seen the way he ran down on me a little while ago, pulling up in the south hopping out a Bugatti and shit…"

"Wait, back up. Ahmani, you're in Georgetown South right now?" he asked, all humor gone from his tone.

I could tell by the look on Amee's face that she could tell that she'd fucked up, but it was too late to eat her words.

"Yeah bruh I…"

"So, Amee, that means your little ass is in the south, too, then," he said angrily.

"Ira, I was just…"

"Shut the fuck up, both of you, because whatever excuse you're about to give is bullshit. Ahmani, you *know* better nigga! Did you tell Amee the latest, or were you just worried about getting your dick wet?"

"I was gonna tell her, but…"

"Don't come at me with no lame nigga shit, bruh. You both got five minutes to be out of the south, and if you think I'm playing then try me," he threatened, hanging up.

"Damn, what the fuck is he so mad about?" she asked.

Before I could open my mouth to explain, my phone started ringing again.

"Tobias, if you're calling to tell me you spoke to Ira, I already know because…"

"No, I'm calling to tell you that your problem just got bigger."

"Now what?" I asked, already dreading his response.

"Your wife just got payment instructions for two hitters to come to town."

Hearing this froze my blood as I looked at Amee and thought about the baby that she was carrying.

"Ahmani, what is it?" she asked.

I knew that I had a decision to make, and it wasn't an easy one.

"Get the taped calls to your people, Tobias. Katrina forced my hand and the only thing that I can think to do is remove her from the equation," I said.

"Are we going with just the phone recordings, or everything right now?" he asked.

"Just the phone recordings for now because I don't want to tip my hand while she's still pregnant."

"A'ight, I got you," he replied, hanging up.

"Baby, what's going on?" Amee asked.

"Katrina's going to jail."

Aryanna

Chapter 18
One week later

For the first few minutes, neither of us spoke, we simply sat there staring at each other. I could feel her eyes trying to do more than probe my thoughts, and if I were guessing I'd say that she was trying to peer into my heart and soul. Even faced with a situation where she had to protect constant strength and toughness, she was still little more than an insecure girl. When she finally picked up the phone in front of her, I still made her wait, needing her to understand who was in control of this situation.

"A week, Ahmani? It took you a whole week to come see me," she said.

"You're lucky I'm here at all."

"Why would you say that to me? I thought you loved me," she said, tears instantly appearing in her eyes.

As badly as I wanted to give up this whole charade, I knew that I still had to play it cool because she was still carrying my babies. With her type of crazy, killing herself and my kids would make too much sense.

"I thought you promised never to hurt me again like you did before," I replied.

"I wasn't trying to *do* that Ahmani! You know that everything that I do is because I love you and our family. Can you say the same?"

"What's that supposed to mean?" I asked.

"Still answering questions with questions, huh? What I mean is I'm still trying to figure out how the police tapped my new phone, the phone that *you* bought me. Unless they had help."

"I see it doesn't take long for paranoia to set in in this place,

huh? Sweetheart, you're incredibly intelligent, but I'll enlighten you since you obviously don't know everything. I
bought *both* of us new phones, but we still had the same old
numbers. Why? That way we didn't have to go through the
hassle of memorizing and giving out a new number. Now as
for the monitoring of your calls, it's to my understand that any
and all surveillance was a part of your bond stipulations. I
didn't sign the paperwork or read the fine print though," I replied.

"So, basically, you're saying that this is all my fault?"

"We all gotta accept responsibility sometime, bae," I said
seriously.

"Does that mean you're gonna accept responsibility for
the part you played in what happened to Robert Cook?"

"Who?" I asked, smiling widely.

"Right. Okay so tell me how this works Ahmani. Are you
just gonna leave your wife, the woman you love, *and* the
mother of your children, in jail to rot? You *know* this is not
good for my pregnancy."

"I'm here ain't I? What do you need me to do?" I asked
patiently.

"Get me out!" she replied through gritted teeth.

"My keys don't fit the particular lock on the doors around
here."

"You think this shit is funny?" she asked.

"No, baby, I *don't* think it's funny, I think it's sad and its
sick, and it was avoidable. How many times do I have to tell
you to *just let me love you!*"

"Ain't that and old Mario song?" she asked, smirking.

"Now who had jokes?"

"Bae, I understand that I have a problem leaving things to
chance, but when it comes to you, I got terrified in a way that
I can't explain. The thought of living without you makes me

want to die a horrible death, because I just can't see any kind of life without you. You've touched my soul that profoundly, can't you understand that?" she asked sincerely.

I knew that if there was ever a time to choose my words carefully now would be it.

"I understand the love you're describing, but baby what you have to understand is that you can't force a natural feeling. You've gotta let go and let god because part of loves beauty is the faith that it takes to sustain it. You gotta believe in me and that my love is built to last because trying to force it can only lead to hate."

"So, you hate me?" she asked, clearly devastated.

"No, I don't. Right now, I feel bad for the things that you've gone through that put you in this situation," I replied honestly.

"But do you still love me, though?"

"Yes," I replied without hesitation.

The relief that she felt was visible in her face and body language, and I was okay with that because it meant less stress on the babies. It was strange to me how I'd had to look at her every day and swallow my hatred, but seeing her now somehow invoked pity within me. She didn't deserve my pity and she didn't deserve my mercy…and I didn't deserve to play god.

"Have you talked to my lawyer?" she asked.

"I spoke with him briefly. Even though you've been given a bond for the two counts of solicitation of murder your bond for the manslaughter charge has been revoked, and your plea has been taken back."

"I bet you're happy about the plea agreement going up in smoke," she said in frustration.

"None of this makes me happy, Katrina, because none of it changes the past, and ultimately all of it will affect the lives of our children."

"We gotta keep that from happening because-."

"No, *you* gotta stop doing shit to *make* that happen!" I replied angrily.

She was smart enough to take her tongue lashing in silence, giving me time to get my emotions under control.

"Your lawyer is trying to move your trial date up so it'll take place as soon as possible, but until then you're stuck in here. Did you need anything?" I asked.

"I need you," she replied softly, putting her hand up to the glass.

I put my hand up opposite hers.

"I'm still here, Katrina, but you gotta stop pushing me away."

"I promise on the lives of our children that I won't do anything else to push you away," she replied solemnly.

"I hope that promise means more than the last one you made me because I'm telling you now that if you break it, it's over between us. For good."

"I won't break my promise, and I'll do everything possible to show you that I truly love you," she replied.

I looked at her for a moment wondering how much of her own lie she actually believed.

"I guess only time will tell," I said.

"I can prove my love for you right now, Ahmani, *and* I can prove that its unconditional."

"How are you gonna do that?" I asked, intrigued, despite knowing that I shouldn't care.

"The days are long in here, Ahmani, but the nights are longer. At night, there's nothing to do and nowhere to run in order to escape the demons and doubts that live in your head.

So, your choices are either go crazy or shine a light in some dark places. I chose the latter."

"Okay," I replied, confused.

"When you didn't immediately answer my calls or come to my rescue, I started thinking all types of things, but mainly I thought about Amee. From the first time I ever saw you two together, I saw the chemistry and it was based off of trust instead purely sexual desire, which meant it had longevity. I could tell that you'd never fucked her, but I know that if you did it would change everything between you two. Call it woman's intuition. I didn't suspect anything though, until you acted like you didn't care where she was when Ira's lawyer couldn't reach her. You'll always care about her, so that statement told me that you knew exactly where she was, and the fact that you lied about it meant that you two were fucking. In that moment of clarity, I had two choices. I could accept it, or I could do something about it. I *thought* that I'd accepted it until I did what I did, but now I know that I've *truly* accepted it. And I still love you."

"Well, don't stop talking now, tell me how you've accepted my *alleged* affair," I said, sarcastically.

"During one of those long nights, I told you about I got the bright idea to hire a private investigator. Now, the fact that her and her son are currently living in *our* house could easily be explained away as your desire to keep her safe given everything that's gone down. But the fact that she's pregnant, *that's* not so easy to explain is it? I don't need a DNA test or a Ouija board to know who her baby's daddy is, and I'm guessing neither do you."

When I'd made my sarcastic comment before, I'd done it with a smirk on my face figuring that she didn't know the one piece of information that she'd just divulged, but I knew that smirk was nowhere in sight now.

Truthfully, I wouldn't have been surprised to find my entire face on the floor at my feet because I damn sure couldn't feel it. Still, I tried to maintain whatever cool I had left.

"So, you know she's pregnant?" I asked.

"I do, and that brings me to the point I made about my ability to prove my love for you in this moment. I'm not angry about her being pregnant. If you want her to live with us in the house in Great Falls, then that's fine. If you wanna give her the old house in Manossas, that's fine, too. Baby, if you want to buy her an entire tower of apartments in Dubai, that's completely okay with me."

"I know I may regret asking this question, but why would you be okay with *any* of that?" I asked.

"Because I know that it doesn't take away from your love for me. The whole time that you've been fucking her you've still been my loving and attentive husband. You've taken care of me emotionally, fucked me proper, catered to my cravings, and been an amazing father to our son, which proves that nothing between you and her had taken away from what we have."

In this moment, I didn't know if I'd suddenly fell down the rabbit hole into her world of crazy, or if the sense she was making was simply appealing to my ego. All I knew was that I was finding it hard to argue with her right now.

"I—us—I don't know what to say," I replied honestly.

"All I want you to do right now is think about how I've done things in the past, and then tell me whether or not I'm proving my love my taking a different course of action."

I wanted to bite my damn tongue off instead of admitting the truth, but in the interest of keeping the peace I chose to man up.

"Yes, Katrina, you've proven your love."

"I'm glad that you see that. All that I ask at this point is that you don't fuck her in our bed because our marriage bed is a sacred thing," she replied.

"I can agree to that. Anything else?"

"I think it would be a good idea if you talked to her because maybe she's not as understanding as I am," she said.

Part of me believed that Katrina was probably counting on that, but I had to admit that she'd done a masterful job of backing Amee into a corner.

"Well played, sweetheart."

"Thank you, my husband," she replied, smiling genuinely for the first time.

"So now what?" I asked.

"Now you hold me down like the real muthafucka I know you are, and we get ready for my trial."

"How is it possible that you still amaze me?" I asked, before I could stop myself.

"Because you keep thinking that you know all there is to know about me, but that knowledge will only come with experience. You got time for me?"

"Somehow I don't have a choice," I replied, shaking my head.

"Now you're understanding."

I couldn't explain the sudden sadness I felt when the deputy tapped her on the shoulder and said that our visit was over, but it was genuine.

"I already put five thousand dollars on your commissary," I said.

"Thanks, bae. Will you come see me again and bring little Ahmani?"

"I think that I can do that," I replied.

"Okay. I'll call you and if you answer you answer, if you don't you don't."

I'd expected some long drawn out declaration of love, but instead she hung up the phone, put both hands on her stomach, and mouthed the words *we love you*. Then she was gone. The whole way back to the car I kept shaking my head trying to figure out what the fuck just happened, but no answer I came up with made sense. I hopped in the Bugatti with the intention of heading straight home, but that somehow didn't happen until two hours later, and I had no idea where I'd been. After sitting in the garage for five minutes I *still* couldn't explain what the hell had happened during my visit with Katrina, which left me wondering how I was gonna explain it to Amee. I thought that I'd simply sneak in the house and go down to the basement for a little while, but Amee being in the kitchen killed that plan.

"Hey, babe, how was your visit with crazy sister-wife?" She asked, taking a punishing bite out of the ham sandwich she was holding.

I had to laugh.

"Don't laugh, I'm hungry," she said defensively.

"That's not why I'm laughing, I was actually thinking about your sister wife comment."

"I'm only joking, baby, so…"

"I knew you were, but you might not be after you hear what I'm about to say," I told her.

"Well, Isaiah is in the pool and Ahmani is sleep, so you have my undivided attention."

I went to the refrigerator to find me something to eat, running the situation down to her in the process. I could tell by the look on her face when I finished that she didn't think a damn think was funny.

"Oh, that bitch really is crazy," Amee stated.

"What was your first clue?"

"So, what did you say?" She asked.

"What could I say, she caught me completely off guard."

"You *should've* told that bitch no, nope, no thank you, ain't gonna happen, and good day. Or you could've had that long overdue conversation about the *divorce* that needs to take place," she said, angrily.

"Baby, I told you that I'm not about to have that conversation while she's still pregnant."

"That's right because you don't wanna stress her, huh? But you're perfectly fine stressing the shit out of me, the woman you love, who's carrying your *miracle baby*. You're really okay stressing me out in my *first* trimester, when the rate of miscarriages is the highest?" She asked hostile.

I could already tell by the look on her face that there was no right answer I could give, so I really didn't know what to say.

"Baby, you're not being fair."

"Fair? So, it's fair for me to forever be your side bitch? I already told you that *ain't gonna happen bruh*!" She stated emphatically.

"Amee, you're not my side bitch, you're my best friend and my heart. I know this is a way more complicated situation than you ever expected to be in, but I promise that I love you and everything will be a'ight," I said, wrapping my arms around her, and pulling her toward me.

She held her body still against mine until I started kissing on her neck the way that she liked.

"You not getting no pussy, Ahmani.

"You sure about that?" I asked, continuing my journey down the side of her neck, and around to her throat.

"Mmm. I'm not giving you none. Good dick won't make m-me forget."

"You're right, baby, it won't, but it'll free your mind of everything else," I said tenderly.

"Okay, daddy, give it to me."

Chapter 19
Two months later

"We the jury find the defendant, Katrina Monroe, not guilty."

Bases on the response around the courtroom I could tell that I was the only one surprised by the verdict. After listening to the state's case for the last few days, I actually thought that Katrina was about to get bammed like any person of color in her situation would've. Obviously, I'd understated the power of a pregnant white woman, even one that was married to a black man. If I hadn't known better, I would've thought that Katrina had bought the jury because it only took them an hour and a half to find her not guilty. The only time I'd seen a jury come back that fast they'd brought a life sentence to someone with them.

"I told you that everything would work out," Katrina said, giving me a hug.

"I believe it was *I* who told *you*," I replied.

"Whatever, you know that the rules of marriage are that the woman is always right."

I opened my mouth to object to this notion, but suddenly her tongue had instigated mine in a heated slap boxing match. It had been months since I'd touched her, let alone kissed her, but the electricity I felt was completely familiar, and just as powerful ever.

"You don't know how *long* I've wanted to do that," she said, pulling back to look up at me.

"Your enthusiasm conveyed it just now, but trust me I know how horny you've been just based on your phone conversations"

She blushed at this reminder of the things said and done between us over the phone in the last couple months, but she still couldn't hide the hunger clouding her blue eyes. I'd told myself that I'd just been doing what was necessary to keep her stable for my children's sake by entertaining her sexual fantasies over the phone, but my bodies reaction to her kiss had me wondering.

"Since I know you didn't walk in here with a gun, I'm guessing that what I feel poking me in my stomach is an indication that you missed me just as much as I missed you," she said, smiling.

In this moment, I was thankful that I was too dark to blush. I decided to switch the focus to her stomach since that was a safer topic of conversation.

"Don't take this the wrong way because you know I think you're beautiful, but, bae, you got *huge*," I said, laughing.

"Thanks a lot, Ahmani," she replied, hitting me and laughing too.

"I'm just saying, I didn't notice it when I came to visit you."

"That's because whenever I pulled my shirt up it was to show you my titties, and they had your undivided attention," she said, giving me a knowing look.

I had no response to give and thankfully her lawyer joining us saved me.

"Well, Katrina, I must admit that I'm glad that you were as stubborn as you were about insisting a trial, even when they tried to make you another offer," Mr. Sprano said.

"I had too much confidence in your capabilities to settle for some bullshit," she replied

"When did they make you another offer?" I asked, confused.

"About a month ago, but it didn't matter because I knew that this was the only outcome that I could live with," she replied.

"Your wife is very determined, Ahmani," Mr. Sprano said.

"Don't I know it. So, if I go pay her bond now, they'll let her out sometime today, right?" I asked.

The two of them exchanged a look that I didn't understand, but I knew that I didn't like it.

"Uh, no, she's actually a free woman right now," Mr. Sprano replied.

When Katrina's eyes met mine, I immediately noticed the guilty expression that she was trying to hide.

"Katrina?" I said, prompting her to speak.

"Bae it's not what you think because I'm not on no type of sneaky shit. It turns out that the cops cut some corners with regards to the legalities involved when it came to that wiretap, so Mr. Sprano was able to get those charges tossed out."

"That's the complete truth, Ahmani, there were no back-room deals made," Mr. Sprano stated.

All I could think was *of course* she got the fucking charges dropped.

"So why didn't you tell me?" I asked.

"Because I wanted to surprise you, baby. I wanted that not guilty verdict to come down, and then I wanted you to sweep me off my feet and take me home," she replied.

She sounded genuine, but in the back of my mind I suspected that she'd wanted to surprise Amee too because she knew that we were still living together. I'd been surprised when Katrina had proven true to her word by not making another move toward Amee or Black Boy, and she hadn't once commented on my relationship with Amee. Today was about to be the biggest test though because now the two female lions would come face to face.

"You definitely succeeded in surprising me. Are you ready to go home?" I asked.

"Oh my, God, you have *no* idea!" she said dramatically.

"Keep her out of trouble," Mr. Sprano said.

"I'll do my best," I replied, taking her hand and leading her out of the courthouse.

"You got a new car I see," she said, eyeing the sparkling 2018 white Maybach with mating white twenty-two-inch-deep dish Pirelli rims.

"It comes with a driver to," I replied, pointing to the short white dude getting out to open the back for us.

"I'm *scared* of you, Mr. Monroe. Don't let the hood find out that you've gone bougie."

"Never that, besides they already know what it is with me." I said, helping her in the car before going around to the other side to get in.

"So, where do you wanna go? Dubai? Paris?" I asked.

"All of those places sound *amazing*, but really I just want to go home bae."

I'd been afraid that that would be her answer, which meant there was no way to avoid what was guaranteed to be a hostile encounter. Amee hadn't softened her position in the slightest in the past two months, which meant absolutely *no sharing*. It wasn't like I couldn't understand her position though, and I was in no way advocating that I be in any type of relationship with Katrina, but there was something about watching my son grow every day that made me understand that my kids had to come first. That meant all my kids.

"Take us home, James," I said to my driver.

Katrina took my hand, but for a while all she did was stare at me.

"What?" I asked

"You're different."

"Well, I am wearing a tailored suit so…"

"No, it's not that, it's you. You're different," she insisted.

"In order for me to understand, I'm gonna need you to be a little more specific than that, bae."

"It's your aura. You've always moved with a certain swag, but its somehow increased and taken on a different edge or maybe it's just polished. Whatever it is, its sexy as *hell*," she said seriously.

I laughed at the expression on her face, despite the look in her eyes that I recognized as the *we're fucking* look.

"Thank you, I guess. I mean it sounds like you were giving me a compliment."

"Oh, I definitely was, and not just because I've been dreaming about you putting that big dick in me either."

Her comment made me quickly put the partition up to keep the driver out of our business, but now we were both laughing.

"Your ass is crazy," I said, shaking my head.

"Crazy about you. I still love you with all my heart, Ahmani, and I pray that you know that."

It was hard to ignore the genuine look she was giving me, but the truth was that even if her love was real it couldn't undo the past. I brought her hand to my lips and kissed the back of it gently before averting my eyes out the window. We rode in silence for a few minutes, and I tried to use the time to sort through the maze of emotions I was faced with. From where I was sitting there didn't seem to be an easy way out.

"What are you thinking about?" she asked softly.

"I've got a lot on my mind."

"How's business?" she asked.

"Business is good. We already broke ground on the daycare center dedicated to my mom and siblings, I bought a couple apartment buildings, and I managed to buy the house right next door to ours in Great Falls," I replied.

"Wow, how did you pull off getting that house from the Bloomfield's?"

"I'm a good neighbor," I said, smiling.

"I *know* you didn't give that ninety-year-old woman no dick because she would've had a heart attack *for sure*."

"Oh, hell nah! I just explained to them that we'd be expanding our family and we wanted to always be near each other," I replied.

"You always did have incredible powers of persuasion Mr. Monroe."

"Right back at you, Mrs. Monroe."

"Well, if business is good then I know that it's the women in your life that are on your mind, and since I'm one of them I think we should talk about it," she said.

"What do you want me to say Katrina? I need a much bigger word than *complicated* to sum it all up, that's for damn sure."

"Let's start with the basics, how is Amee's pregnancy going," she asked.

I looked over at her to see if she was being serious and I was pleasantly surprised to find no malice or maliciousness on her face.

"Her pregnancy is fine and the baby is healthy," I replied.

"Do you know what you're having?"

"No, we want it to be a surprise," I said.

"You know, after our first conversation at visit I never asked you if you talked to her about what we discussed…did you?"

"Yeah, I did," I replied shortly.

"Okay, so then I can assume that based on the lack of a follow up conversation between you and I that she wasn't thrilled with the idea. I bet you think that puts you in a hell of a situation, huh?" she asked.

"That's putting it mildly."

"Then you're not being real with yourself, Ahmani."

"And how do you figure that?" I asked, trying not to catch and attitude.

"Because the reality is that you'll never be done with either of us now that we're having your kids. I've seen the way you are with Little Ahmani, and you're a *wonderful* father, but I also know what your relationship was like with your mom. If for no other reason than that, you're gonna want all your kids to have the best relationship possible with their mothers. If I hadn't beat the charges against me and had actually had to go to prison, I had no doubt that you would've made sure our kids had a relationship with me. No matter how much a part of you hates me."

"Katrina, I…"

"It's okay, I know you hate me on some level, I mean you'd have to with all the fucked-up shit I've done. I know that you love me too though, even if you can't admit that to Amee, or yourself sometimes. Love is action, bae, and it's not something that can be faked for as long as you've been demonstrating with actions that you love me. I'm sure that you love Amee, too, and that love comes without the complications of hate. The problem is that it still doesn't take away from our love, nor does it erase the family that we've built. What *you* have to realize is that neither of us are going anywhere because if you can't realize that you can't convince Amee to accept it."

I could tell she was looking at me to say something, but no words passed in between my lips. In my brain, I was asking myself why the fuck she was making so much sense all of a sudden! I felt like I might be losing my goddam mind because I *knew* she was cray-cray, but if I was agreeing with her logic then that made me…what? Most likely in need of a muthafuckin' cat scan!

"I'ma be real with you, I'm gonna need time to process what you just said to me because it's a lot to take in," I said.

"I understand, I'm not going anywhere. Can I make a request, though?"

"What's that?" I asked.

"A bitch had been *feigning* for some barbecue, so do you think we can make a stop?"

It felt good to laugh again after such a serious and intense conversation, and the longing in her eyes provided the necessary comic relief. I gave the driver directions to what would forever be known as our restaurant, but instead of going in for a take-out order we actually grabbed a booth to eat in. I'm not sure if it was her intent or not, but suddenly we found ourselves on a date. The most surprising part of me was that I was actually enjoying myself because this reminded me of a different time in our lives to be so young and not together for that long, it seemed like we'd gone through a lifetime of shit. Most of the time the members of bad shit overshadowed the good things, but every now and then the good things were allowed to come through and be remembered. Kind of like a rainbow in a storm. Before I knew it, we'd spent two hours talking and laughing while playfully fighting over barbecue ribs.

"I gotta admit, freedom looks good on you because some days you had me worried," I said truthfully.

"You've been on the inside so you know what it's like, just like you know how good it feels to be out."

Thinking about when I'd got out of jail took my mind directly to the activities that we'd engaged in that same night in her Jeep. The close quarters hadn't been the only thing that was tight. I could tell by the grin on her face that she was having the same thoughts that I was, and I knew how dangerous that was for both of us.

"Tell me something, did you get your pussy ate while you were in there?" I asked.

"Why you all in *my* business, I didn't ask you if you were getting your dick sucked out here," she replied laughing.

"Fair enough."

"Would it have bothered you if I did?" she asked.

"Nah, I mean you've never mentioned an attraction to women, but I wouldn't trip."

"Oh, okay, so if it was a male officer, you'd have a problem," she stated.

"I…"

Somehow, I couldn't tell the lie about not caring either way because the thought of a nigga sticking dick in her while she was pregnant with *my* babies had me heated.

"Relax, Ahmani, no man has or will have any part of my body ever again. It's *all yours*. To answer your question, though, my cell mate was kind of cute."

"How the hell does that answer my question?" I asked, calming down a little.

For a moment, she simply stared at me with that mischievous twinkle in her eye.

"You didn't," I said, smiling.

"No, I didn't. She did, though."

"You so *nasty*!" I whispered fiercely, laughing.

"You can judge me all you want, but you *know* how necessary it is for me to release right now. I mean phone sex with you was great and all, but thinking about you would have me laying on my back, panties *soaking wet*. You didn't want me to suffer did you, baby?"

The sexy voice she'd suddenly turned on me, along with the look in her eyes, was making my chest tight and my dick hard.

"I mean nah, I get it. I ain't mad," I replied.

"She was good but nobody has ever eaten my pussy better than you," she purred seductively.

"Don't start no shit, woman."

"Whatever you say, daddy," she replied, smiling.

Thankfully the waitress picked that moment to bring the check, allowing me to divert my attention. Once we had our doggy bags, I escorted her back to the car.

"James, why don't you run in and get something to eat for yourself, its good food," I suggested.

"Thank you, sir," he replied, heading toward the restaurant.

"Is it gonna bother you if I smoke?" I asked, once we were back in the car and I was rolling a blunt.

"No, I'm just mad that I can't join you. You best believe that as soon as I drop your daughters though I'm blowing a pound to the face."

"So, you not breastfeeding?" I asked smiling.

"You're the only one I want sucking on these titties bae. Unless Amee wasn't to join in."

Her comment stopped my blunt in mid roll as I turned to look at her.

"I'm sorry, did you just offer to have a *threesome*?" I asked in disbelief.

"Of course, I did, are you seriously gonna tell me that the thought didn't cross your mind?"

"Actually, it didn't because I didn't think that was something that you'd *ever* fo for," I said honestly.

"Surprise!"

She'd rendered me speechless, so I went back to twisting my blunt and lighting it.

"Mmm, that smells good, what is it?" she asked.

"Watermelon-mango Kush, and it's *everything*."

"Bae, you know science has proven that weed is-."

"You're not getting none. Nice try," I said, trying not to choke.

The pout she fixed on her face didn't move me and I proved that by blowing a cloud of smoke in her face.

"Thanks for the contact high."

"You're welcome," I replied chuckling at her salty tone of voice.

"Tell me something, Ahmani, does Amee suck dick better than me?"

I choked instantly, which of course made her laugh with delight.

"You're not funny," I said.

"I wasn't trying to be, it was a serious question."

"Oh, so you want a serious answer? You sure about that?" I asked, staring her in the eyes.

"I'm sure, keep it one hundred with me, bae."

I knew that there were three ways to answer this question, and the longer I took the more the weed influenced one answer in particular.

"I don't remember," I replied.

"You don't remember *what*?"

"I don't remember what your head game is like," I said, hitting my blunt again.

"I see. It has been awhile, huh?"

"Even as she asked this question, she was reaching for the zipper to my pants. Within seconds, she had my dick free and she was caressing it with the gentleness reserved for something sacred.

"May I?" she asked.

"You never asked before, why start now?"

"The difference is in the fact that I've truly submitted to you as my king, and so it is your will that I will obey," she replied, increasing the pressure of her hand.

"Damn, you know what to say," I said, pushing her hand into my lap.

I didn't wrap my hands in her hair like I normally would, I simply let her go for what she knew while I kept smoking. From the beginning her movements were bold, deep throating me with speed and enough force to take my breath away. It didn't take long to figure out that I couldn't smoke while she did me this way, and I put my blunt out. When James got back behind the wheel and pulled off this only seemed to motivate her more because now, she was literally falling face first on the dick.

"Katrina," I moaned, trying to prolong my climax.

She made it clear that she was having none of it though, and within minutes my cum was hitting the back of her throat with the pressure of a busted fire hydrant.

"Do you remember now?" she asked, leaning back and picking up the remainder of my blunt.

"Uh-uh huh," I replied weakly.

I wanted to tell her not to light my shit, but it was too late. She hit it a few times, and then passed it back to me while putting my dick away for me. Before I knew it, we were gliding to a stop in front of our house, but I wasn't ready to go in. One look at her and I could tell she was faded. It wasn't her temperament that I was worried about, though.

"Come on," she said, taking the blunt from my hand and stepping out of the car.

I followed her lead, knowing I needed to be in between her and Amee. Somehow the weed had me convinced that the house was big enough to hide Katrina from Amee, but of course, Amee and Isaiah were in the kitchen when we walked in.

Chapter 20

"How the fuck did *you* get out?" Amee immediately asked.

"A jury of my peers," Katrina replied, smiling.

"Oh, so everybody was crazy as shit. That makes sense," Amee said.

"Isaiah, now might be a good time to go check on Little Ahmani," I suggested.

"I don't know, I ain't seen my mom beat nobody up in a while so I should probably stick around."

"Isaiah, go," Amee said forcefully.

I could tell by the disappointment on his face that he really expected this to be a shit show, but I was hoping to avoid that.

"Amee," I said, hoping she would heed the warning in my tone.

"Yes, my husband?" she replied, looking directly at Katrina.

I was positive she was looking to bait her, but Katrina just snickered as she finished the blunt and tossed the roach down the sink.

"What type of mother smokes weed while she's pregnant?" Amee asked.

"One whose spent countless hours reading about the pros and cons of marijuana. Do you read, Amee?" Katrina asked innocently.

The flame in Amee's green eyes had been smoldering, but it shot to white hot instantly, causing me to step directly in front of her.

"Chill," I demanded.

"You better talk to her, Ahmani, because you already know that I ain't the one," Amee said.

"I don't get you, Amee. I mean, I let you and your son stay in my house, I even let you bounce up and down on my husband's dick, but I haven't come at you with any hostility, so what's your beef?" Katrina asked.

"My beef is that you ain't shit, bitch, and you don't deserve, Ahmani! I, on the other hand, do deserve him. So, yeah, I've been living in your house and I've been riding his dick *and* face, but not because you *allowed* me to. I did it because Ahmani is *my* man."

"The way he eats pussy is magical ain't it?" Katrina asked, giggling.

I could tell her nonchalance was only further pissing Amee off, but I was sure that was Katrina's intention.

"Look, it's obvious that you two can't talk, so why don't you go to separate ends of the house," I suggested.

"That's fine with me because I could use a bath and..."

"I'm not staying under the same roof as this bitch, are you crazy?" Amee yelled at me.

"Amee listen..."

"You could always stay in that house across the way since I heard that we own it now," Katrina offered.

"Bitch *you* go stay across the way, *I'm* staying with my man," Amee declared.

"Technically, he's our man, but I'd be more than happy to set up a roaming nightly schedule so we get an equal amount of dick. Well, it might not be equal because I don't know if you can take it like I can, but you understand what I'm saying," Katrina replied calmly.

I could tell that the calmer Katrina got the more infuriated Amee became.

"Ahmani, it's time that you really straighten this crazy bitch because it's obvious the last two months in County made her even more delusional. I know that you wanted to spare her feelings because she's pregnant and not all there mentally, but this shit has gotta stop."

I knew what I was supposed to say in this moment, but for some reason the words couldn't find their way up my throat and out of my mouth.

"Uh oh, sounds like he may have been trying to spare *your* feelings," Katrina said, laughing.

"Shut up, Katrina," I stated.

"You better do more than tell that bitch to shut up, nigga, set her ass straight."

"Yo, who are talking to?" I asked, looking at Amee.

"I'm talking to *you,* nigga! I already told you what it was so…"

"And I already told *you* what the fuck it was, and at no time did I say that *you* get to dictate to *me* how to handle this situation," I said angrily.

"Ahmani, that's not what I'm trying to do, but obviously she thinks you feel something for her that you don't and now is the perfect opportunity to let her know what's real."

"Trust me, sweetheart, you have no *idea* what he feels for me," Katrina said.

Now it was Amee who smiled with confidence.

"He *hates* you, Katrina. He hates everything about you except those babies you're carrying and trust me if it wasn't for them, your stinking ass would've *been* dead! You need to step out of your dream world and realize you're responsible for killing his *family* so he could *never ever* love you again. If he ever truly did."

I could feel Katrina moving behind me, but when I turned to prevent whatever attack she was planning, I saw something that startled me. Katrina was genuinely smiling. When Amee saw the look on her face, her own smile actually faltered a little bit and she shuddered like there was a chill in the air.

"You actually believe everything you just said, huh?" Katrina asked.

"As strongly as I do in the Gospel," Amee replied.

"Okay, then, I guess there's only one way to find out. Ask him," Katrina said.

"Bitch, I don't need to ask because…"

"Oh, no, but you do. You do need to ask him. Ask him if he hates me. If he hated pulling his dick out and jacking off for me during our visitation. Ask him if he hated the phone sex, or even the late-night conversations where we discussed everything and nothing. Ask him if he hates that I just *blew his mind* in the backseat of that Maybach when I had him moaning as his cum flowed down my throat. Go ahead *Little Amee*, ask him," Katrina insisted.

The look on Amee's face morphed from disbelief to suspicion to anger, and finally settled on devastation.

"Ahmani…" Amee said.

I knew I could deny all the shit Katrina had just said, but Amee knew me well enough to see through the bullshit. That meant all I had in this moment was the truth.

"Amee, its complicated, but you know I love you," I professed.

The way she shook her head sadly told me she didn't know anything like that.

"You can't have us both, Ahmani, it'll never work," Amee said.

"It will if you try," Katrina said, taking a non-threatening step toward her.

"I assure you, Amee, I eat pussy better than Ahmani does."

"What's *wrong* with you? Why would you be okay with sharing your husband with anyone else?" Amee asked.

"Because I love my husband, and I only want to make him as happy as he's made me. I look at it as enhancing both of our lives, plus someone to share the work load in the bedroom ensures we stay fresh enough to keep shit interesting. You gotta ask yourself, would you rather have half of a good man, all of a bad man, or no man at all," Katrina replied.

The look on Amee's face said she thought the woman in front of her was speaking a foreign language she was incapable of comprehending."

"I'd rather have the man that I was promised, so me and my son will be going next door," Amee said.

"Amee wait…"

"Isaiah!" she yelled.

"You don't gotta do this," I said, taking her hand in my own.

"I'm only doing it because I love you, but I meant what I said, Ahmani, you can't have us both. I suggest you don't take too long with your decision or you might find yourself by yourself," Amee stated.

I wanted to say anything I had to in order to convince her to stay, but as soon as Isaiah came into the kitchen, she grabbed the spare house keys off of the wall and left.

"I'm going to take a bath," Katrina said, leaving me with just my own thoughts for company.

My mind and my heart were literally in knots and me pulling in opposite directions. I grabbed the keys to the Bugatti on my way to the garage, hopped in the car, and took off.

I knew the situation I'd put myself in was beyond the therapy that a long drive could provide, and that's why I had a specific destination in mind.

I made it to the jail just before visitation cut off. And since there were only a hand full of people, I was sent upstairs to the visiting area immediately.

Ten minutes went by before he showed up, but the relief I felt was worth the wait.

"What's up, Pops?"

"What's going on, young nigga? I wasn't expecting you," he replied.

"I know. I should've come sooner, but life has been crazy out here."

"Yeah your brother has been keeping me up to date. Seems like you stepped in it with both feet this time, huh?" he asked.

"Pops, you don't even know the half of it."

"Well, I'm sure that's why you came to see me, so let's hear it," he said patiently.

For all the times I'd lacked the words to put this whole mess into perspective, I suddenly came down with a case of word vomit, and it all poured out.

Old Man Doug sat and listened, sometimes laughing, sometimes scowling, but never interrupting. When I was done with the run down, he just stared at me.

"Well?" I asked.

"This would make one hell of a movie."

"Tell me about it. What do I do, though, Pops?" I asked seriously.

"Ahmani the most important thing in this whole mess is your kids, and they're the ones that you have to protect so your life's ugliness doesn't affect them. I can't tell you how to do that, but I can tell you that you need to figure it out *quickly*. And buy some condoms with your tender dick ass!"

I knew he was serious, but we still had a good laugh. I felt like it was much too soon when they signaled that our visit was over, but I felt a little better.

"Do you need anything, Pops?"

"Nah, young nigga. I'm good to go, and I only got a short time left," he replied.

"I'll be there when that door opens for you."

"I'm counting on it," he replied, smiling before hanging up the phone and disappearing.

When I left the jail, I drove around aimlessly but it didn't take long for me to realize I couldn't avoid the inevitable.

By the time I pulled into the garage, it was dark outside, and I could see the lights on in the house next door. As badly as I wanted to go to Amee, I knew I had to give her at least tonight to calm down. I knew it would be weird for both of us, though, because we hadn't slept apart in months.

I'd expected to find Katrina in the kitchen trying to eat everything including the marble, but instead I was forced to follow the smell of pizza to our bedroom.

"Damn, was this the munchies or a craving?" I asked, looking at her sitting naked in the bed with three large pizza boxes around her.

"A little bit of both, but I'm willing to share."

After taking off my suit jacket and shoes, I climbed in the bed next to her and grabbed a piece of pepperoni pizza.

"Did you have clothes on when the delivery boy came?" I asked.

"Maybe."

I quickly reached over and pinched one of her nipples hard.

"Ouch! Yes, I had clothes on damnit!" she said, hitting me.

"Just making sure."

"Where did you go anyway?" she asked, picking up another piece of pizza, and biting it in half.

"To get some advice about what to do about my crazy ass life."

"How'd that work out for you?" she asked, chuckling.

I reached over and pinched her nipple again.

"Ahmani, stop, that shit *hurts*!"

"I'm sorry, bae, come here I'll kiss it and make it feel better."

Pizza still in hand, she moved closer to me and offered me her swollen tittie, with its hard nipple. I put my pizza down and slowly licked a circle around her nipple before pulling it in between my lips and gently sucking. When I pulled back, I found her slack jawed with a mouth full of pizza and her eyes closed.

"Careful or you're gonna choke," I warned, laughing.

"Why did you stop?"

"I didn't know that I was supposed to keep going," I replied.

"Are you not attracted to me because I'm here now?"

"Baby, why would you say some shit like that? You know you'll always be sexy to me," I said sincerely.

"Will you make love to me, then?"

"On top of the pizza?" I asked, smiling.

She may have been eight months pregnant, but I had to give her props for how fast she got the bed cleared off. I could tell that she was focused, too, because she didn't bring a single slice of pizza to bed with her. I stood up and slowly undressed, watching her watching me with a famished look in her eyes.

"How do you want it?" I asked, once I was naked.

"From the side," she replied, quickly turning over and putting her juicy ass my way.

I climbed back in the bed, becoming the big spoon to her little spoon, pushing my dick inside of her nice and slowly.

"Oh, God I missed you," she whispered, holding onto me tightly.

"I missed you, too," I replied, kissing her neck while giving her insides a thorough exploration. I could feel the need in her body because she was already moving with me, matching me stroke for stroke, but she was so tight I feared hurting her if I gave her all of me.

Without warning her pussy gushed, allowing my dick to tap the bottom of her well with each blow.

"Fuck! Ahmani!"

"Take this dick, bae. You…"

"Stop! Stop!" she cried suddenly.

"Really, after one orgasm?" I asked surprised.

"That wasn't an orgasm, my water broke."

Hearing this brought the dick all the way out of her and had me hurdling her body to get to the phone.

"Oh shit-oh-shit-oh shit, just breathe, baby," I said, trying not to panic as I got 911 on the line.

"I'm breathing, but *goddam* it hurt!"

Once I had the ambulance on the way, I hurriedly put some clothes on and helped her into a maternity dress. The contractions were still pretty far apart, but when one hit, I felt like I was in the clutches of a three headed monster! I don't know how I managed to get us both downstairs in one piece, but by the time I got her to the couch the paramedics were knocking on the door.

Within three minutes flat, Katrina was strapped to a stretcher, we were in the back of the ambulance and on the move.

"Ah—Ahmani, I'm not ready for this," she said, crying.

"Baby, you got this, and I'm right here with you. I'll be here every step of the way."

"Promise!" she screamed, putting my hand in a punishing grip as another contraction hit.

"Aww, shit! Yes, yes, I promise!"

She clutched my hand tightly, again. I was sure I'd never regain feeling in my right hand.

"Ahmani. Ahmani, I want a C-section," she said, once they had her in the delivery room with her legs spread wide.

I looked at the doctor and she shook her head to let me know that these bundles of joy were coming the old fashion way.

"Uh, baby, I don't think a C-section is an option right now."

"But I want it," she whined.

"Just relax the epidural will kick in before you give birth, and all you'll feel is a little pressure," the doctor said.

"But my pussy will look like roast beef," Katrina replied, crying again.

I could hear the doctor chuckling behind her mask, and I had to fight to keep a straight face.

"Katrina, please just focus on bringing our babies into this world healthy because that's all that matter. I'll still love you if your pussy looks like lunch meat."

"Promise?" she asked sincerely.

"I promise."

I had to make her a few more promises as the night wore on but finally after eight hours, our two beautiful baby girls came kicking and screaming into the world. The miracle of child birth was simply amazing and beyond all words, but I was truly happy that I hadn't embarrassed myself by fainting.

"You know, we've never discussed names," I said, holding the older of our two girls.

They'd only come two minutes apart, but I had no doubt that she would forever remind her sister of it.

"I chose their names a long time ago," Katrina replied, gazing lovingly at my other daughter.

"Oh, really? Well, thanks for letting me know."

"I guess I was worried that you wouldn't approve," she said.

"Try me."

"Well since you're holding the oldest, I thought we'd name her Kendra and this little beauty would be Keisha," she replied softly.

There were too many emotions overwhelming me to speak, but I managed to nod my head in acceptance.

"We need to get mommy cleaned up, and while we're doing that dad can go with the nurse to make sure the right baby gets the right name," the doctor said.

"Identical twins, wow," I said, still in awe.

"I love you, Ahmani," Katrina said.

I walked over to the bed, leaned down, and kissed her tenderly.

"I love you, too, bae."

Once the nurse had Keisha, I followed her to another room where both babies were weighed and measured. After that, it was off to the room where the rest of the babies were, and I stood there like every other proud father watching my girls first moments in life. It may not have been manly to cry, but I did it anyway. It took me almost an hour to pry myself away from the glass, but I knew I needed to check on Katrina. I expected to find her sleeping peacefully after the ordeal she went through, what I *didn't* expect was to walk into her room to find Amee holding a gun to her head.

"What the fuck are you doing?" I asked in a harsh whisper.

"I'm doing what you *won't* do, I'm taking this bitch with me and getting rid of her for good."

"Amee listen…"

"Listen my ass, Ahmani, you know that this is what needs to happen."

"I get it, she needs to be out of our lives, but I've got a plan," I said quickly.

"What plan?" Amee asked, unconvinced.

"I've got all the evidence needed to send her to prison, just hold on. I'ma call the cops right now," I said, pulling out my phone.

I could see the hurt written all over Katrina's face, but right now it was either jail or death.

"Ahmani, you can't..."

"Shut up, bitch! I told you he's mine," Amee said, smacking her with the pistol.

"Amee, just chill, I got a plan."

"I don't have faith in your plan. Ahmani, just put the phone down."

"But, Amee, it'll work," I said, preparing to dial.

The sound of her cocking the hammer of the pistol froze my fingers because out of my peripheral, I could see the gun had moved. It was aimed at me now.

"Do you love me, bae?" Amee asked.

"Of course."

"Then put the phone down, and don't make me tell you again..."

To Be Continued...
Bae Belongs to Me 3
Coming Soon

Submission Guideline

Submit the first three chapters of your completed manuscript to ldpsubmissions@gmail.com, subject line: Your book's title. The manuscript must be in a .doc file and sent as an attachment. Document should be in Times New Roman, double spaced and in size 12 font. Also, provide your synopsis and full contact information. If sending multiple submissions, they must each be in a separate email.

Have a story but no way to send it electronically? You can still submit to LDP/Ca$h Presents. Send in the first three chapters, written or typed, of your completed manuscript to:

LDP: Submissions Dept
Po Box 870494
Mesquite, Tx 75187

DO NOT send original manuscript. Must be a duplicate.

Provide your synopsis and a cover letter containing your full contact information.

Thanks for considering LDP and Ca$h Presents.

Coming Soon from Lock Down Publications/Ca$h Presents

BOW DOWN TO MY GANGSTA

By **Ca$h**

TORN BETWEEN TWO

By **Coffee**

BLOOD STAINS OF A SHOTTA **III**

By **Jamaica**

STEADY MOBBIN **III**

By **Marcellus Allen**

BLOOD OF A BOSS **V**

By **Askari**

LOYAL TO THE GAME **IV**

LIFE OF SIN II

By **T.J. & Jelissa**

A DOPEBOY'S PRAYER **II**

By **Eddie "Wolf" Lee**

IF LOVING YOU IS WRONG… **III**

LOVE ME EVEN WHEN IT HURTS **III**

By **Jelissa**

TRUE SAVAGE **VII**

By **Chris Green**

BLAST FOR ME **III**

A BRONX TALE III

DUFFLE BAG CARTEL III

By **Ghost**

ADDICTIED TO THE DRAMA **III**

By **Jamila Mathis**
LIPSTICK KILLAH **III**
Mimi
WHAT BAD BITCHES DO **III**
A HUSTLER'S DECEIT 3
KILL ZONE **II**
BAE BELONGS TO ME III
By **Aryanna**
THE COST OF LOYALTY **III**
By **Kweli**
SHE FELL IN LOVE WITH A REAL ONE **II**
By **Tamara Butler**
RENEGADE BOYS **III**
By **Meesha**
CORRUPTED BY A GANGSTA **IV**
By **Destiny Skai**
A GANGSTER'S CODE **III**
By **J-Blunt**
KING OF NEW YORK IV
RISE TO POWER III
By **T.J. Edwards**
GORILLAZ IN THE BAY III
De'Kari
THE STREETS ARE CALLING II
Duquie Wilson
KINGPIN KILLAZ IV
STREET KINGS 2

Hood Rich

STEADY MOBBIN' **III**

Marcellus Allen

SINS OF A HUSTLA II

ASAD

TRIGGADALE II

Elijah R. Freeman

MARRIED TO A BOSS II

By Destiny Skai & Chris Green

KINGS OF THE GAME II

Playa Ray

BLOOD STAINS OF A SHOTTA I & II

By **Jamaica**

LOYAL TO THE GAME

LOYAL TO THE GAME II

LOYAL TO THE GAME III

LIFE OF SIN

By **TJ & Jelissa**

BLOODY COMMAS I & II

SKI MASK CARTEL I II & III

KING OF NEW YORK I II,III

RISE TO POWER I II

By **T.J. Edwards**

IF LOVING HIM IS WRONG…I & II

LOVE ME EVEN WHEN IT HURTS I II

By **Jelissa**

WHEN THE STREETS CLAP BACK I & II III

By **Jibril Williams**

A DISTINGUISHED THUG STOLE MY HEART I II & III

LOVE SHOULDN'T HURT I II III

RENEGADE BOYS I & II

By **Meesha**

A GANGSTER'S CODE I &, II III

By J-Blunt

PUSH IT TO THE LIMIT

By **Bre' Hayes**

BLOOD OF A BOSS **I, II, III & IV**

By **Askari**

THE STREETS BLEED MURDER **I, II & III**

THE HEART OF A GANGSTA I II& III

By **Jerry Jackson**

CUM FOR ME

CUM FOR ME 2

CUM FOR ME 3

CUM FOR ME 4

An **LDP Erotica Collaboration**

BRIDE OF A HUSTLA **I II & II**

THE FETTI GIRLS **I, II& III**

CORRUPTED BY A GANGSTA I, II & III

By **Destiny Skai**

WHEN A GOOD GIRL GOES BAD

By **Adrienne**

THE COST OF LOYALTY

By Kweli

A GANGSTER'S REVENGE **I II III & IV**

THE BOSS MAN'S DAUGHTERS

THE BOSS MAN'S DAUGHTERS II

THE BOSSMAN'S DAUGHTERS III

THE BOSSMAN'S DAUGHTERS IV

THE BOSS MAN'S DAUGHTERS **V**

A SAVAGE LOVE **I & II**

BAE BELONGS TO ME I II

A HUSTLER'S DECEIT I, II, III

WHAT BAD BITCHES DO I, II

By **Aryanna**

A KINGPIN'S AMBITON

A KINGPIN'S AMBITION **II**

I MURDER FOR THE DOUGH

By **Ambitious**

TRUE SAVAGE

TRUE SAVAGE II

TRUE SAVAGE **III**

TRUE SAVAGE **IV**

TRUE SAVAGE **V**

TRUE SAVAGE **VI**

By **Chris Green**

A DOPEBOY'S PRAYER

By **Eddie "Wolf" Lee**

THE KING CARTEL **I, II & III**

By **Frank Gresham**

THESE NIGGAS AIN'T LOYAL **I, II & III**

By **Nikki Tee**

GANGSTA SHYT **I II &III**

By **CATO**

THE ULTIMATE BETRAYAL

By **Phoenix**

BOSS'N UP **I , II & III**

By **Royal Nicole**

I LOVE YOU TO DEATH

By Destiny J

I RIDE FOR MY HITTA

I STILL RIDE FOR MY HITTA

By **Misty Holt**

<u>LOVE & CHASIN' PAPER</u>

By **Qay Crockett**

<u>TO DIE IN VAIN</u>

SINS OF A HUSTLA

By **ASAD**

<u>BROOKLYN HUSTLAZ</u>

By **Boogsy Morina**

<u>BROOKLYN ON LOCK I & II</u>

By **Sonovia**

<u>GANGSTA CITY</u>

By **Teddy Duke**

<u>A DRUG KING AND HIS DIAMOND I & II III</u>

<u>A DOPEMAN'S RICHES</u>

<u>HER MAN, MINE'S TOO I, II</u>

<u>CASH MONEY HO'S</u>

By Nicole Goosby

<u>TRAPHOUSE KING **I II & III**</u>

<u>KINGPIN KILLAZ I II III</u>

<u>STREET KINGS</u>

By **Hood Rich**

<u>LIPSTICK KILLAH **I, II**</u>

<u>CRIME OF PASSION I & II</u>

By **Mimi**

<u>STEADY MOBBN' **I, II**</u>

By **Marcellus Allen**

<u>WHO SHOT YA **I, II**</u>

Renta

GORILLAZ IN THE BAY **I II**

DE'KARI

TRIGGADALE

Elijah R. Freeman

GOD BLESS THE TRAPPERS I, II, III

THESE SCANDALOUS STREETS I, II, III

FEAR MY GANGSTA I, II, III

THESE STREETS DON'T LOVE NOBODY I, II

BURY ME A G I, II, III, IV, V

A GANGSTA'S EMPIRE I, II, III

Tranay Adams

THE STREETS ARE CALLING

Duquie Wilson

MARRIED TO A BOSS...

By Destiny Skai & Chris Green

KINGS OF THE GAME II

Playa Ray

BOOKS BY LDP'S CEO, CA$H

TRUST IN NO MAN

TRUST IN NO MAN 2

TRUST IN NO MAN 3

BONDED BY BLOOD

SHORTY GOT A THUG

THUGS CRY

THUGS CRY 2

THUGS CRY 3

TRUST NO BITCH

TRUST NO BITCH 2

TRUST NO BITCH 3

TIL MY CASKET DROPS

RESTRAINING ORDER

RESTRAINING ORDER 2

IN LOVE WITH A CONVICT

Coming Soon

BONDED BY BLOOD 2

BOW DOWN TO MY GANGSTA